Chase the Dead

A Detective Ryan Chase Thriller, Volume 4

M K Farrar

Published by Warwick House Press, 2022.

This is a work of fiction. Similarities to real people, places, or events are entirely coincidental.

CHASE THE DEAD

First edition. August 30, 2022.

Chapter One

The lights of the Clifton Suspension Bridge appeared as little more than smudges of orange and yellow against the fog. Only the first few feet of the metal struts were visible, the top part vanishing into the white. The murky waters of the River Avon below were impossible to see, swallowed by a combination of darkness and the bad weather.

The dipped headlights of cars appeared out of the gloom like spaceships in a science fiction film, but the girl stayed back, pressing herself to the grey stone walls of the side of the bridge. Voices filtered through to her ears, but they were young and filled with laughter—definitely not how the person she was meeting here would sound.

She envied these strangers. It felt like a long time since she'd laughed that way. It was all her own fault. She'd opened Pandora's box and now she couldn't shut it again.

No, that wasn't necessarily true. Maybe she could put things right. She wanted that more than anything—to eradicate these past few months and start over. She'd made some bad choices and said things she now regretted, but that didn't mean they couldn't come to some kind of agreement.

She sucked in a shaky breath, trying to still her nerves.

It would be okay.

She checked her phone for what seemed like the hundredth time that night, reassuring herself that nothing had changed. A part of her hoped for a message to say the person she was meeting wouldn't be coming after all, but if they didn't, nothing would be resolved. The same issue that had been keeping her awake, night after night, wouldn't have gone away.

She paced back and forth a couple of times, wringing her hands in front of her.

Maybe she should just leave.

It wasn't worth it.

But the idea twisted her stomach.

What felt better—staying or going? Neither option felt like a win. If she left, she risked everyone finding out, but if she stayed...

The thud of footsteps approaching was muffled in the dark. A shape moved through the fog. Automatically, she retreated, plastering her back to the damp coolness of the wall. It was ridiculous hiding—they knew she was here—but instinct kicked in.

The footsteps continued, brisk, determined. Someone on a mission to get somewhere without wasting any time. Could it be them?

A figure formed in the fog, and she froze, but they passed straight by, apparently unaware of the teenager in the tiny dress—an outfit completely unsuitable for the weather—standing only a matter of feet away. She wrapped her slender arms around her torso, goosebumps standing out on her skin. She should have worn a jacket.

Her heart beat so fast, it seemed to be tripping. Her fingers itched to check her socials, get that reassurance from her friends that everything was normal. They were all bitching about life, complaining about parents or friends, or teachers they thought were bullying them. But their simple lives managed to simultaneously make her feel better while also filling her with rage. They thought they had problems because someone was talking about them behind their back, but they seriously had no idea what a real problem was. She'd give anything for that to be the biggest issue in her life.

She suddenly became aware that she was no longer alone. Someone stood to her left, and she spun to face them.

The combination of the dark and the fog meant it took her a moment to realise who it was. A mixture of nerves and relief filled her.

"You came."

Chapter Two

The body of the teenage girl lay bent and broken on the outcropping of limestone rock that made up the Avon Gorge. The trees and bushes only went partway to sheltering the body from the view of those above.

Standing on the Somerset side of the Clifton Suspension Bridge, DI Ryan Chase put his hands on his hips and shook his head. It was always worse when they were so young. The position of the body was hard to access, and the sergeant in charge of the scene had called in the Avon and Somerset Search and Rescue to help retrieve her. They couldn't risk anyone else falling, but it made things difficult as far as processing the crime scene went.

"Sergeant Banner," Ryan said, recognising the squat police officer in charge of coordinating the scene. They'd worked together on previous cases, including the one where body parts had been found in the river now passing below them. "Good to see you again, though obviously I'd prefer it to be under different circumstances. What do we know so far?"

"The victim has already been identified as seventeen-year-old Tai Moore. She'd been reported missing by her mother, Lorraine, shortly after midnight, so when the girl's body was spotted by a jogger, who called nine-nine-nine, it didn't take long to figure out who she was. The last proof of life we currently have is when her mother saw her leave the house at about ten past seven yesterday evening. She could have died any time between then and the early hours of this morning."

Ryan peered back over the edge of the bridge. "I don't envy either of us this crime scene. It's not an easy one as far as access goes."

"You're not wrong on that front. We're assuming she originated from the bridge, but we can't know that for sure just yet."

The bridge had been closed in both directions, the outer cordon making up the end on the Leigh Woods side, and also the area directly below where the body had been found.

Movement caught Ryan's attention, and he turned as his sergeant, Mallory Lawson, walked briskly towards him. She'd already pulled on protective outerwear over her trouser suit. Ryan noted her dyed black hair had recently been cut in a sharp bob at her jaw, and her fringe was even shorter than normal.

"Morning," Mallory said to both men. "Any idea what happened yet?"

Banner shook his head. "Not yet. There's a possibility she was a jumper, but there's also the chance she was pushed."

"Any witnesses?" Ryan asked.

"So far, only the jogger, fifty-two-year-old Thomas Dignam, who first spotted the body." Banner pointed up to a camera mounted on the wall opposite where they were standing. "I'm hoping that will give us a good idea of what happened."

"It's working?" Ryan checked.

"According to the bridge's management team, all the cameras were recording last night."

Mallory frowned. "They're not owned by the council then?"

Banner pursed his lips. "Nope. It's a private company, and the cameras have all been updated to thermal imaging surveillance recently, too. They deliver a high-contrast picture to the bridge's security office where they're monitored by Clifton Suspension Bridge attendants."

She raised both eyebrows. "They're not monitored very well if something like this was allowed to happen and no one reported it."

Banner shrugged. "It was foggy last night, and obviously dark as well. I believe the thermal imaging cameras will still have worked, despite that, but I don't know how good they are."

"We're going to need to talk to whoever was on shift last night and obviously get a copy of that recording," Ryan said.

He paused to take in the scene again. The Clifton Suspension Bridge sat high above the River Avon. It was quiet considering it should have been rush hour. Uniformed officers and response vehicles blocked both sides, and traffic had been diverted into the city via the A369. Though the girl's body had been discovered a hundred feet down, there was no denying the possibility that she may have originated from the bridge and it would be considered a crime scene as much as the area where the body itself had been discovered.

From the damage to her body, the most obvious assumption was that she had fallen from the bridge. The question was, did she jump or was she pushed?

"Has anyone informed the family?" Mallory asked.

"Yes," Banner said. "I sent a couple of officers around as soon as we got a positive ID."

She blew out a breath and shook her head. "God, her poor parents."

"It's just the mother, I believe." Banner wrinkled his nose. "The father hasn't been on the scene for some time."

Ryan took his phone out of his jacket pocket. "I'll send DCs Quinn and Kharral to interview the mother. I'll get them to take a look around the victim's bedroom as well, try to get an idea about what sort of person the victim was. I'll also ask them to keep an eye out for any signs of a note."

"A suicide note?" Mallory confirmed.

Ryan nodded. "It's probably not how it's done these days—using a pen and paper, I mean. It's more likely that she'd have posted something on social media, but you never know." He looked to Banner. "Any sign of the girl's phone?"

"Not yet, but if it was in her pocket and it fell out after she jumped, or was pushed, it could have landed anywhere."

They all glanced down at the rough terrain beneath them, the wide but slow-moving brown river to their left, and the railway track between the river and the crime scene. Members of the search and rescue team moved carefully around the body.

"We're probably going to have to bring divers in if it doesn't show up." Ryan didn't envy them that job. Trying to find a small rectangle of metal on a sludgy riverbed was the proverbial needle in a haystack. "We'll request her phone records anyway. They might give us an idea about what she was doing here. Did she come to meet someone voluntarily? Or did someone bring her here?"

"Someone could have thrown the phone in the river to ensure it wouldn't be found, at least not right away," Mallory suggested.

"Something we'll definitely consider once we know a little more about the events surrounding her death." Ryan turned back to Banner. "Did you run a check on the witness?"

"Yes, but he's clean. No priors, and no reason to suspect him, except that he's the one who reported the body. He's with one of my officers in the response car."

Ryan glanced in the direction of the vehicle. "We'll need to talk to him."

"I can do that," Mallory volunteered.

"Thanks."

There was a sudden thrum of activity as the search and rescue team used a winch to lift the victim's body, already encased in a body bag, up onto the bridge. It made more sense to bring her up rather than down. The pathway on this side of the river, that ran along the bottom of the gorge, wasn't great for access, and they'd needed to bring in numerous vehicles.

He spotted one of the city's pathologists, Nikki Francis, among the team. Her normal glasses had been replaced by a pair of tinted ones, to combat the glare of the morning sunshine, and her blonde hair was hidden beneath the white protective outerwear. She was easily recognisable, though, at least to him, by the confident and forthright manner in which she conducted herself. They'd had some flirtation and a date a little while back, but it hadn't gone anywhere—mainly because he hadn't been in a great place, mentally, at the time, but also because he was still hung up on his ex. He doubted she had given him much thought since, but he still felt slightly awkward whenever he was in her company. He wondered if he owed it to her to tell her about Donna, but would that just be rubbing salt in the wound? Or would she be happy for him? Or not think it was her business one way or the other?

In the end, he decided not to mention it. It was hardly the time or the place to talk about his personal life.

He went to where she stood over the gurney containing the body bag.

"I'd say good morning," he said, "but they never are when they start like this."

She didn't offer him a smile, but he wasn't offended. These were sombre occasions, especially when it involved a young girl, as this one did.

"I'd like to get a look at her before she's taken to the morgue, if that's okay," he continued. "Might give me a head start on the case."

It was frustrating that he hadn't been able to properly view the body in the position she'd been found. Right now, it was just their best guess that she had originated from the bridge, and that she had been alive when it had happened, but he couldn't ignore the possibility that this was a cover-up. The girl might have been killed somewhere else and her body thrown from the bridge to make it appear as though she'd jumped.

The search and rescue team were well equipped to deal with crime scenes and had taken photographs and bagged up any potential evidence, but it wasn't the same as being hands-on himself. He liked to stand in the position of the victim, to drink up every detail around him, to put himself in their place as they'd died and try to see through their eyes.

But he was also aware that the search and rescue team didn't need him attempting to abseil off the side of the bridge and most likely get himself into trouble doing so. He hadn't done any sort of abseiling or climbing since he'd been to a residential with his old school over thirty years ago and he still remembered how even back then he'd stood on the edge of the cliff face with his knees knocking and thighs trembling, certain he was going to make an idiot of himself in front of his school friends. They'd all jeered and hooted, perhaps partially in encouragement but also in jest. Even though he hadn't wanted to do the abseil at the time, peer pressure had forced him over the edge and down to the bottom. Ryan didn't much fancy the thought of repeating something similar, only now as an adult, closer to fifty than forty in age, and surrounded by his colleagues. He'd never live it down at the station.

Nikki nodded. "Of course." She unzipped the body bag to reveal a brown-skinned girl with tight black curls creating a halo around her face. There were multiple bruises and contusions on her skin. "We've formally ID'd her by a small tattoo on the inside of her wrist that her mother gave as an identifying feature, and that she's still wearing a gold necklace with a heart on it, which her mother also told the police about when she reported her missing."

Ryan noted the full face of makeup, though Tai's young skin didn't need much. She was dressed as though she was going out somewhere. False eyelashes, tiny dress, black Doc Marten boots. It didn't look like the sort of outfit someone would wear if they planned on killing themselves, but then maybe she'd hoped to leave a pretty corpse.

"I know it's still early days," he said, "but have you got any thoughts around what you can make of her body so far?"

"From what I can see, I'd say the injury patterns are consistent with that of a fall from a great height."

"You don't think she was killed and then moved?" he checked.

Nikki twisted her lips. "It's possible, but the amount of blood around the body tells me her heart was still beating when she hit the rocks. I won't know for sure until I've done a full post-mortem, however."

"Any estimation how long she's been dead?"

"As you know, it's not an exact science, and it's getting warm early at this time of year, but I'd say she was most likely there overnight. Her body is cool to touch, and rigor mortis is already setting in."

"Are we looking at a few hours? Or longer."

"I can't give you a definite answer to that, Ryan, especially not before doing a full post-mortem."

"Okay, thanks anyway."

It was frustrating not having a better idea of when she might have jumped, or fallen, or been thrown from the bridge, but he hoped the CCTV footage would give them a definitive answer. He didn't know what the footage would be like, given that it had been both dark and foggy, but he hoped it would be good enough to spot the victim. Of course, without a better idea of what time she'd died, they'd still have hours of footage to go over to try and spot her.

If she'd left home just after seven, she could have been killed any time between shortly after then, to the early hours of the following morning. That was still a lot of time to cover.

Nikki zipped the body bag back up, hiding the victim's damaged face.

"You'll come down to the morgue when I'm ready for the post-mortem?" she asked.

Ryan nodded. "I'll be there."

Chapter Three

M allory left Ryan speaking with the pathologist and approached the man sitting in the back of the response vehicle. It was parked a short distance from the end of the bridge on the Somerset side, a uniformed police officer standing close by.

Sitting sideways on the back seat, his white trainers planted on the ground, was the man she took to be Thomas Dignam. A set of bony bare knees sprouting dark hair protruded from a pair of shorts. His head was bent, and a bald spot in the centre of his scalp betrayed his age.

Mallory lifted her ID to show the uniformed officer.

"I'd like a word," she said.

The officer nodded. "He's all yours."

Right now, Thomas Dignam was simply a witness, but there was always a possibility he had something more to do with the victim's death. It wasn't unheard of for a witness to be involved in a crime. With him being a white male, in his early fifties, she couldn't ignore the possibility that Thomas Dignam might also be a suspect. Some people liked to play these games, believing they were smarter than the police, wanting to be right there to watch the investigation going on around them. They got a kick out of it, and it wouldn't be the first time a witness became a suspect, but for the time being, she needed to keep her mind open.

Unless, of course, the girl had jumped.

Suicide was one of the leading causes of death in young people. While men and boys were three times more likely to kill themselves than their female counterparts, that didn't mean that girls didn't also take their own lives. It was a complex matter that stemmed from multiple different issues that affected a young person's mental health. They might have academic pressures or worries. They might have been experiencing abuse or bullying, at school or in the home. There could be substance abuse involved.

These were all things they'd need to look into when it came to unravelling the events surrounding Tai Moore's death.

"Excuse me, Mr. Dignam?" she said.

The man lifted his head from his hands and nodded. "Yes, but it's Tom, please. Or Thomas. I'm happy with either."

"I'm DS Lawson." She showed him her ID as well. "I understand you found the girl's body?"

He nodded again.

She continued. "I realise you must be feeling pretty shaken up after seeing that, but I need to ask you some questions."

"I know. Your colleague said it was a good idea for me to stick around until you'd spoken to me."

Mallory gave the uniformed officer a nod of thanks. She'd question him as well once she was done with Thomas Dignam, see if there was anything the man had said initially that perhaps didn't fit with his current account. When people were in shock, their memories could do strange things.

Mallory took out her phone to record the conversation.

"Before we begin, I do have to let you know that I'm going to record this conversation for my records. You are entitled to have a solicitor with you, if you so wish."

He shifted anxiously. "I'm not under arrest, am I? I haven't done anything wrong."

"Not at all," she assured him. "I just have to make sure you're aware of your rights."

"I am," he said, "and I don't have anything to hide. I don't need a solicitor or to go down to the station."

"In which case, we'll begin." She got his full name, date of birth, and address. "And what do you do for a living, Tom?"

"I'm an accountant." He gave her an apologetic smile. "I know it sounds boring to most people, but I enjoy it."

"How long have you been doing that for?"

He huffed out a breath. "God, pretty much since I qualified twenty years ago."

"Are you married?"

"Yes, seven years now. We have two children, a boy and a girl. My wife stays home with them."

"Can you run me through exactly what happened in the time before you found the girl's body? Start from when you got up."

A small frown marked his brow. "Umm, I woke up about five-thirty, which is normal for me. I got dressed in my running gear and left the house."

"Did anyone see you leave?" she asked.

"No. I try to sneak out without disturbing anyone."

She gave him a smile. "Does that always work?"

He returned the expression. "No, not always. The kids are still small and like to get up at the crack of dawn, but I prefer it if I can let my wife sleep in a little. You know what they say: happy wife, happy life."

"I can see the sense in that." Mallory brought the conversation back into focus. "Do you often run this route?"

"Sometimes, yes. Other times, I head towards the park instead."

"What made you decide to go this way today?"

He shook his head. "I have no idea, but I wish to God I hadn't. No one needs to find something like that first thing in the morning." He seemed flustered. "I mean, I'm glad the poor girl was found, and I don't wish the horror of finding her on anyone else, but I still would rather it hadn't been me."

"It's okay," she assured him. "I'm sure most people would feel exactly the same way. Can I ask you to think back to the minutes before you found the body. Did you see anyone else around?"

He twisted his lips as he thought. "Well, there was traffic on the bridge, just like there is most of the time."

"What about anyone on foot? Was there anyone lurking around? Anyone who might have caught your attention?"

"No, it was early."

"Okay, thanks." She considered her next question. "In order to see the body, you must have stopped on the bridge and looked over the side. What made you do that?"

"My shoelace came undone." He gestured at the pair of expensive Nikes on his feet. "I stopped and used the wall to brace my foot against it so I could do the laces back up, and while I was there, I thought I'd catch my breath and check out the view. That was when I saw her."

"What did you notice first?"

"Her legs sticking out and the boots she was wearing. I thought maybe it was a drunk or a homeless person just lying there. It wasn't until I took in what I was seeing a bit more that I realised both her legs were at weird angles, like they were broken. I was already using my phone because I listen to a podcast app when I'm running so I called nine-nine-nine."

He juddered his knee up and down as though he was nervous.

Mallory checked her notes. "And that was at thirteen minutes past six, is that correct?"

"Sounds about right."

When she got back to the office, she'd have to check the route he claimed he'd taken, with the average pace he ran, to make sure the timings all added up. Maths didn't lie. If there was time missing, he'd need to account for it.

He cleared his throat. "Do you know who she is yet?"

"We believe so, but obviously we're not releasing that information until the family have been informed." She thought they already *had* been informed, but he didn't need to know that.

"Of course."

Mallory took one of her business cards out of her pocket and handed it to him. "I think that's everything for now, but we might need to speak to you again at a later date. And if you think of anything you haven't mentioned already, my number is on that card. Can I get one of my colleagues to drive you home?"

He shook his head and got to his feet. "No, thanks. I think I'll run. I could do with clearing my head."

"I understand. Thanks for waiting around to speak to me."

Tom Dignam nodded and turned away from her, taking off in a slightly unsteady jog.

Chapter Four

Ryan returned to Sergeant Banner, who was instructing a couple of his officers. There was no point in going back into the office until they'd spoken to the bridge attendant who'd been on that night.

He told the sergeant so.

"We held on to him," Banner said, "though he's made it clear he'd prefer to go home. Kept saying his shift had finished and that he'd been up for hours, which I appreciate, but considering a young girl has been killed, I didn't think it was much of a sacrifice to ask him to lose a couple of hours' sleep."

"Did he mention seeing anything?" Ryan asked.

"No, and he was pretty defensive about it. I got the feeling that was more because he couldn't have been doing his job properly rather than him being involved, but you never know. He'll be able to send over the footage from the security cameras as well."

"Good."

Mallory was still caught up in other things, so he went to the security office alone. It was located a distance from the bridge, so Ryan had to leave the immediate vicinity of the crime scene to speak to him.

He entered the building, keeping an eye out for signs for the office. He spotted a uniformed officer standing outside one of the doors and jerked his chin in a nod.

"I assume I'm in the right place. I'm after the security attendant who did the shift last night."

"Bob Newton," the officer said. "He's in there. Not happy about it either."

Ryan grinned. "He'll probably be even less happy after spending time with me."

"His shift replacement turned up." The officer jerked his chin towards a man in his twenties with a buzzed haircut—he had that air of ex-military about him—sitting on a plastic chair farther down the hallway, his head bent over his phone. "But I thought it was better if he didn't touch anything until after one of your team had spoken to Mr Newton."

"Good thinking. Thanks."

Ryan knocked on the door and entered without being invited. He found himself in a small, windowless room. One wall was covered in security monitors. A couple of chairs sat facing the screens, and one of them contained the man Ryan was there to speak to.

Bob Newton was a grouchy-looking man with a bald head and the kind of eyebags that really only came from a combination of age, poor genetics, and night shifts. He remained slumped in his chair, not bothering to rise to greet the detective.

"Don't get up," Ryan said, though Bob didn't show any signs of doing so. "I'm DI Chase and I'd like to have a word." Ryan showed the other man his ID and took the seat opposite him. "I'm sure you're aware that the body of a teenage girl was found on the gorge, just below the bridge first thing this morning. It's my understanding that you were on duty last night, Mr Newton."

He sniffed. "Yeah, that's right. I was supposed to have gone home ages ago. The plods out there wouldn't let me go."

"I'm sure you understand the reason why my colleagues requested for you to stay. I'd like to ask you some questions about last night, if that's all right?

"I don't really have much of a choice, do I?"

"You're not under arrest, Mr Newton. You're free to leave at any time, but since you're possibly one of the only people who may have witnessed what happened last night, I'd certainly appreciate your cooperation. A young girl is dead."

Newton sighed and folded his arms even tighter across his chest. "Better get on with it then so I can get home and get my beauty sleep."

Ryan thought no amount of sleep could fix Bob Newton. "What time did your shift start last night?"

"Ten, and I was supposed to have finished at seven."

"So, that's an nine-hour shift. Is that how long you normally work?"

"Yeah, it is. We have an hour overlap for handover."

"Were you in the office all night?" Ryan asked.

"With the exception of the few times I went to take a leak or grab something to eat, yes, I was."

"How much attention do you pay to all of these?" Ryan waved a hand at the bank of monitors.

There were twelve different screens, all showing various areas of the bridge, including the barriers where people in vehicles had to pay one pound in order to cross. Other parts of the bridge weren't so easily recognisable however—all metal struts—and he realised he was viewing the structure underneath the part of the bridge people walked and drove over. One of the screens also pointed towards the area where the bulk of the investigation was taking place—the spot where the girl must have either jumped or been pushed from. It looked like normal CCTV to him, though he was sure Sergeant Banner had mentioned that they'd had thermal imaging cameras installed recently.

Bob shrugged. "As much as I need to."

"You can't be watching them all the time."

"I guess not."

Bob pushed a paperback—the cover well-worn, with a spaceship on it—under the desk with his foot.

"But you do watch them closely?" Ryan asked, noting the paperback.

The man's gaze flicked up to the right. "As closely as I need to."

"Yet you didn't see the girl go over the wall?"

"I might have been taking a piss then."

Ryan had a feeling Bob wasn't watching the screens at all when he was working and instead had his nose buried in his book. He couldn't say he blamed him, after all, it must be hard being here alone, hour after hour, while the rest of the world slept on. Ryan had pulled his share of night shifts, but he normally had plenty of colleagues around him to keep him going.

Bob cleared his throat. "Anyway, there are digital alarms that sound if someone is where they shouldn't be, so I don't need to be staring at them all night."

"No alarms went off last night, though?"

"No. They only go off if someone is on a part that's not accessible by the public. If the girl fell from the wall, they wouldn't have gone off then. Honestly, the new cameras are an improvement, but I don't think they're really there for the protection of people."

Ryan frowned. "What do you mean?"

"The bridge is a Grade One listed structure. We're here to protect it from damage, both malicious or accidental. The older cameras made it harder to see anything at night or in bad weather, especially with the glare from the lights of the bridge itself, but these new ones work on thermal imaging, so we can see if someone is where they shouldn't be."

"But no one caught your eye as being somewhere they shouldn't be last night?"

"No, sorry."

Ryan took out the notepad and pencil that he always preferred to use to take notes. "Are you able to give me the times when you weren't watching the cameras?"

Bob stared at him. "Are you kidding me?"

"Not at all. We still don't know what time the girl died, and we're going to need to go through all the footage taken from last night." He motioned at the screen where the images of the police officers moved around. "Since it's clear you had an excellent view of the spot where the girl either jumped or was pushed, I assume you were using the bathroom at the time she died, so if you could narrow those times down for me, I'd appreciate it."

His cheeks grew mottled with red. "I don't know that."

"You have no idea? I mean, when was the last time you left this room to use the toilet?"

"When my shift was almost finished. Sometime after six."

Around the same time the jogger called triple nine, Ryan mentally noted.

"And the time before that?"

He shrugged. "God, I don't know. A couple of hours before, I guess."

Ryan lifted an eyebrow. "So four a.m.?"

"Sounds about right."

"And before then?" Ryan prompted.

Bob's gaze shifted away. "Dunno, maybe an hour or so before."

"That's a lot of bathroom breaks."

"Look, when you get to my age, the bladder isn't quite what it used to be, okay? Be grateful that you don't have to experience it yet. I can barely get through an hour or two without my bladder telling me it needs emptying again. Enlarged prostate, the doctor says, but nothing more heinous just yet. Got to keep an eye on it, though."

"I'm sorry to hear that."

Ryan felt bad for ribbing him about the toilet breaks. Of course, it could just be a cover and Bob Newton knew and saw exactly what had happened to Tai Moore and was just using an enlarged prostate to cover his tracks.

"Is there anyone else on site who can confirm you were here all of your shift?"

"No, but the cameras here will be able to show you that I was."

"Do you have the authority to release all the footage from last night right up to this morning to us? I'll need it sent to me at this email address." He handed Bob Newton his card.

"I'll need to get it signed off by my boss, but I can do it. When do you need it by?"

"As soon as possible."

"I guess that means I won't be finishing my shift anytime soon," he muttered.

"Sorry about that. I'm sure the dead girl's family will appreciate your sacrifice," Ryan said.

Bob at least had the decency to look guilty.

Ryan got to his feet. "Myself or one of my colleagues may need to speak to you again after we've reviewed the footage, so please don't go leaving the country or anything."

"Can't go abroad on my wages," he complained.

Ryan left him to it. He was glad to get out of the man's company. While Ryan knew he wasn't exactly a barrel of laughs himself at the best of times, he hoped he wasn't that miserable to be around. Someone who dragged everyone else down around him. No wonder Bob Newton worked alone.

He returned to the crime scene and caught up with Mallory. "Anything interesting to report?"

She shook her head. "Not so far. The jogger's story checks out, though I'll go over his timings from when he said he left home to when he called triple nine. What about the bridge attendant?"

"He claims to have not seen anything."

"Even though it's his job?"

"Says he must have been on the toilet when the girl went over."

Mallory rolled her eyes. "Jesus. Are you buying that?"

"I'm not sure. I mean, there's always the possibility he was the one who pushed the girl from the bridge. Maybe he saw her on the security monitors, hanging around, and went to investigate. There was an altercation of some kind, and she fell over the wall?"

"Does he seem the type?"

"I'm not sure. He doesn't have any priors or any reason for us to suspect him. I've requested the footage from the office as well, so we'll be able to see if he left his post for any length of time around when she died. The cameras are infrared, so even though it was most likely still dark and foggy when Tai died, they'll still have caught something."

Mallory frowned. "Infrared? Doesn't that mean the image will be just colours—like reds and oranges, depending on the body heat?"

"No, they switch to black and white at night. They're definitely not as clear as CCTV would be in the middle of the day, but it's surprising how much detail they show. Plus, you have to remember that if it had been CCTV that was still being used, we wouldn't have caught anything at all. The combination of the glare from the lights on the bridge, the dark and the fog, would have left us with nothing."

She gave him a half-smile. "I guess we should be grateful they were changed then."

"Let's wait until we see the footage before we come to that conclusion."

Chapter Five

"Where are we going, Mum?"

Faye took her eyes off the road for a moment to glance over at her seventeen-year-old daughter. "I told you. I'm not sure yet. We just have to keep moving."

Chloe let out a long sigh and rested her forehead against the passenger window.

"You've got rid of your phone, haven't you?" Faye double-checked.

"I told you that I had."

Faye wanted to believe her daughter, but she knew how much that bloody phone meant to her. It felt as though Chloe thought she didn't even exist if she wasn't able to Snap or Instagram or TikTok something. Not Facebook, though. As Chloe had often pointed out to her, Facebook was for Facebook mums—whatever that was supposed to mean. Faye just took it as that particular social media app was no longer considered cool.

They each had a small suitcase in the boot, containing the items they'd both grabbed from their drawers first thing that morning. It was sad to think that was what made up their possessions now—a few hastily packed toiletries and clothes. Faye thought of her lovely house and everything it contained and choked back tears.

Her daughter hadn't given up on her complaints. "God, I'm so bored."

"Seriously, Chloe?" She darted a glare at her, biting down on her urge to tell her to shut the fuck up. She was still trying to be a good mother, despite everything. Because she had failed, hadn't she? She must have failed at her job as a parent for this to have happened.

Chloe sank lower in her seat, her long blonde hair falling over her face.

Guilt swamped Faye for snapping. Chloe blinked back tears, and Faye's guilt solidified.

She reached out a hand and took her daughter's, squeezing it tight. "It'll be all right. I promise."

Chloe sniffed and wiped her face. "You can't promise that."

"No, you're right, I can't."

"We can't be on the run forever, Mum. What are we supposed to do for money? Where are we going to live? What about my exams?"

"You should have thought of that before..."

She clamped her lips around the words, cutting herself off. It wouldn't do either of them any good to start laying on the blame game. If they were going to get through this, they needed to stick together.

Faye took a deep breath, trying to steady herself. "Just remember the plan."

"I know, Mum. It's just not going to be easy. I'm going to miss my friends—"

"I don't care how much you miss them, you're *not* to get in touch, do you understand?"

"People are going to talk. They're going to ask questions. Isn't it better that I'm in touch and say I'm going on holiday or something?"

Faye arched an eyebrow. "In the middle of college?"

"Okay then, we'll say that an aunt is sick and we have to take care of her. Doesn't that make more sense? Just vanishing like this isn't going to work."

"If you're in touch with people, they'll be able to track you down. They'll use your phone location, or you'll mention something that they'll be able to use, or you'll send a photograph with the picture of something recognisable in the background. The only way no one will be able to find us is if we vanish."

Chloe sighed again.

A combination of anger and fear and frustration rose inside her again, and she tightened her fingers around the steering wheel, her knuckles turning white. "I'm doing this for you, Chloe. Do you think I want to run away from my life? My friends? My job? I have a life, too." Her voice had risen in pitch as she'd spoken, until it was high and wavering with emotion.

At some point, people were going to notice them missing. Who would report them? She wasn't sure—her work, most likely, or Chloe's college.

She was going to have to get rid of the car. If someone spotted it, it would give them an idea about which direction they'd travelled in and what location they'd ended up at. When the police started looking for them, would they be able to pick up her licence plate on the cameras? If so, should she try and change it somehow? She knew doing so might cause unwanted attention from traffic police, so it would be a gamble. She'd deliberately taken all the tiny, windy backroads in the hope to stay off the radar, but the time would come when she'd need to get fuel, and she was sure all the garages had cameras these days.

They needed somewhere to stay that night, somewhere no one would know them. She'd never before realised how much she'd relied on the internet until she found she didn't want to leave a trace of herself using it. Chloe hadn't been the only one to have to get rid of her phone.

An old-fashioned bed and breakfast, that's what she needed. Somewhere the owners would be grateful for the business and wouldn't ask too many questions if she and Chloe appeared at the front door.

"Sorry, Mum," her daughter said. "You know I never meant for things to end up like this."

Guilt twisted inside her again. Chloe had made mistakes, but she was still only a kid, even at seventeen.

"We just need time, Chloe, that's all. Time for things to be safe again."

Chapter Six

B ack at the office, Ryan called his team together in the incident room.

The two constables who'd gone to Tai's mother's house had already returned. DCs Linda Quinn and Dev Kharral had had the horrible job of trying to gather whatever useful information they could while dealing with a grieving parent. It wasn't easy, questioning someone whose world had just been torn out from under their feet, but it was necessary. All too often, family was involved in the death of a loved one, and they wouldn't be doing their jobs as detectives if they didn't look into the kind of relationships the family had with the victim.

Linda Quinn was the older and most experienced member of the team, having worked for the police force for going on thirty years now. She was great with the general public, her warm nature putting them at ease. People opened up to her when they might not with someone younger. Dev Kharral was more stoic but had an excellent eye for detail, so together, Ryan could trust they'd get all angles covered.

He attached a photograph of Tai Moore to the wall, together with images of her body and the location it had been found. He doubted there would be anyone in the room who didn't instantly know the area. The Clifton Suspension Bridge was a famous landmark.

One by one, his team entered. Most were clutching mugs of tea and coffee—they'd all had an early start. Chatter passed between them, though the conversations weren't necessarily about the same thing. Conversation in the office could be as much about what they'd watched on the television or how the family were doing as it was about the crimes they investigated each and every day.

Ryan waited until everyone had found a seat and settled down and then did a roll call to ensure everyone was present.

He got started.

"At thirteen minutes past six this morning, we received a triple-nine call from a jogger, Thomas Dignam, to say he'd seen the body of a young female on the gorge below the Somerset side of the Clifton Suspension Bridge. The body was quickly identified as seventeen-year-old Tai Moore, who was reported missing by her mother, Lorraine Moore, just after midnight.

"As I'm sure you're all aware, the weather was bad last night. We had a thick fog that might have hidden Tai and whoever she was with from any passers-by, and also from anyone who drove past while she was there. Luckily for us, the CCTV system used on the bridge has been updated recently to infrared cameras which won't have been affected so badly from either the fog or the fact it was most likely dark when she either jumped or was pushed. Unfortunately, the location of the body has made reaching it difficult, and we had to call in the Avon and Somerset Search and Rescue team to help us retrieve it. Getting SOCO down there is also proving to be an issue. We have, however, been able to shut off the bridge, so scenes of crime officers can work on the area we believe she must have been before she'd fallen."

Ryan paused to take a sip of his lukewarm coffee.

"At the time of her death," he continued, "Tai was wearing a short red dress and a pair of black Doc Marten boots. She was identified by a gold heart necklace she was wearing and a small tattoo on her wrist."

"It wasn't warm last night," Linda said. "Didn't she take a coat?"

"Doesn't look like it. Double-check with her mother in case the coat's gone missing somewhere along the way. She might have left it somewhere."

One of the other DCs, Craig Penn, shook his head, his lips pursed. "These girls go out half naked and post pictures of themselves online in barely anything at all, and people have to act shocked when something bad happens to them."

DC Shonda Dawson's mouth dropped open, and she twisted in her seat. "Umm, victim blaming much over there? It's not the girls' fault that some men seem to think girls and women only exist to provide them with something. Girls should be allowed to wear and act however the hell they want without fear of being raped and murdered by men. Women aren't the problem here."

Craig sat back. "I get that, but let's be honest, that's simply not the world we live in, is it? There has to be a little bit of self-awareness going on. I mean, you wouldn't throw yourself in front of a car and then wonder why you've been run over."

Shonda raised both eyebrows. "You're comparing men to cars? Seriously?"

"All right, calm down, both of you," Ryan said. "Let's focus on what matters here, and that's finding out what happened to Tai."

Shonda Dawson and Craig Penn were the younger members of his team. Craig could get a bit cocky sometimes, and Ryan had needed to have the occasional word with him about coming into the office, clearly hungover. But Ryan remembered what it was like to be in your twenties, with no real responsibilities. It was easy to go and hang out in the pubs with all your colleagues and have one—or more—too many pints. Sometimes Ryan had to remind himself that his own rigid control over everything in his life wasn't the same for everyone. But it was how he managed his OCD, though the controlling aspects were probably just another symptom. If he drank the same thing, went to bed at the same time, did his routines in the right order, then the other, more debilitating things such as checking a door was locked over and over, were more manageable.

Ryan continued. "Currently, we believe Tai was last seen by her mother, leaving her house at ten past seven yesterday evening, but that might change as we learn more about Tai's final movements. Tai told her mother she was meeting friends, but as of yet we don't know who. That's something we definitely need to find out. Did she meet anyone, and if so, who, because we need to talk to them? We're going to want to request CCTV footage of all the surrounding streets, both of her house and those leading up to the bridge, see if we can work out which route she took and if she was with anyone at the time.

"Tai's house is located here," he pointed at the spot on the map with the end of his pen, "in Brislington. As you can see, that's a substantial way from where her body was found. It would have taken her approximately an hour and a half to walk between her house and the bridge. Did she use public transport? She doesn't hold a driving licence yet, so if she got to the bridge by car, someone else drove her. Could it have been the same person who killed her? We don't even know for sure just yet if she was even still alive when she was brought to the bridge. She might have been killed elsewhere and thrown from the bridge to make it look as though she jumped, but we'll know more once we've received the post-mortem results." He paused and took another sip of his coffee. All the talking was making his throat dry. "We need to request her bank records, see if she stopped in at any shops on the way and used her card. If something comes up, we'll need CCTV footage from the shop as well."

His boss, DCI Mandy Hirst, slipped into the room and took a seat near the back. She gave Ryan a nod of acknowledgment but didn't interrupt.

He took a couple of paces, using the movement to think. "I want to know everything there is to know about what kind of person Tai Moore was. Did Tai have a boyfriend? Girlfriend? What were her interests outside of college? Did she have a part-time job? Who are her real-life friends, and where does she hang out? I want to know every detail about her life. I also want to know what her movements were up to the moment she died. What was Tai doing between shortly after seven p.m., when she left her house, and the time she died?"

Shonda asked a question. "Any idea what time she might have died?"

"Currently, we're looking somewhere between nine p.m. and the early hours, but hopefully, we'll know more precisely once we get the CCTV footage in."

Shonda wrote it down in her notes.

"We're going to need to go over all her social media," Ryan said, "see if we can get an idea of who she was. Was anyone giving her any grief on her socials? What about her DMs? Girls of this age live a lot of their lives online. Currently, we're still searching for Tai's mobile phone. Her mother says she had it with her when she left the house and believes she wouldn't have left it anywhere. Like any other teenage girl, she treated it like a lifeline. Unfortunately, the large drop between the bridge and where her body was found means the phone could have fallen anywhere, assuming it did fall with her and someone didn't take it. The search and rescue team are aware that it's missing. We need to request her phone records, see if we can get a ping off a local tower, so we know for sure that she had it with her."

Dev lifted his hand briefly. "Tai's mother allowed us to take Tai's laptop, so it's with digital forensics now. She didn't know what her password might be, but that shouldn't cause a problem."

"Good." Ryan nodded. "That might make up for the fact we don't yet have the phone."

Ryan looked to Linda Quinn and Dev Kharral. "You both went to speak to the mother first thing. How did it go?"

Linda answered for them both. "She was devastated, understandably, but she wasn't alone. There's a boyfriend on the scene—not the girl's boyfriend, the mother's. He's been living with them for the past ten months."

"What was the relationship like between Tai and the mother's boyfriend?"

"Fractious, apparently. They didn't get on. He only came into their lives twelve months ago, and they've butted heads on a number of occasions. Lorraine fights with him about parenting her, too. He oversteps the mark, tries to act as though he has some kind of say in Tai's behaviour, which obviously never went down well with Tai."

Ryan grimaced. "No, I bet it didn't."

"He's younger than the mother as well, quite significantly so. She's forty-one, and he's only twenty-nine."

"What's his name?"

"Richard Foyle. Current address is the same as Tai Moore's."

Ryan slowly formed a picture of what family life must have been like. "I can understand why Tai wouldn't want to be parented by him then. Is there any chance there's more to the relationship than that?"

"You mean was there something romantic between Richard and Tai?"

"Or abusive," Ryan added.

She sighed. "Honestly, I don't know, but I don't think we should rule it out."

"What's his background look like?" Ryan asked.

Dev Kharral took over, checking his notes. "Here's where it gets interesting. I ran a check on him, and he has a history of drug charges. Even served time for supplying cocaine a few years back."

"Is there a possibility Tai was using drugs? Maybe she got herself caught up with the wrong people?"

He made a mental note to make sure Nikki Francis did a full tox screen on Tai. If there were drugs in the teenager's system when she'd died, he wanted to know about it.

"It's a line of enquiry we definitely need to follow. We've got a lot of people we need to interview and a lot of CCTV footage that needs to be gone over, so I'm going to need everyone on the case."

"Boss," Linda said, "are we treating this as a murder case or a suicide?"

"Until we get the footage from the bridge, to find out if Tai was alone or not at the time of death, we're going to have to keep our minds open."

"How long is that likely to take?"

"It's been requested, so I'm hoping it'll be sent over any minute now."

Ryan looked around at his team, lining up the actions for the day with which members would be best to carry them out.

"Dev, can you go through the footage from the bridge cameras as soon as it comes through. We're going to have to check more than just the camera pointed at the spot where we believe Tai fell from. If someone dropped her off on the bridge, they would have paid the toll, and their licence plate would have been caught on camera."

Dev nodded. "If that's the case, then we'll have got lucky. We'll definitely need to check out any licence plates of vehicles coming and going late yesterday evening, though. One of the drivers might have seen something, despite the fog."

Ryan agreed. "Absolutely. Every vehicle crossing the bridge around the time she died is going to need to be checked."

"I can help with that," Craig volunteered. "There's going to be a fair amount, so if we divide it between us, we'll get through it quicker."

"Okay," Ryan said. "You're going to have to start at around seven-thirty p.m. as we know Tai couldn't have got to the bridge much before then, and go right through to six a.m., to when the body was found. We're watching out for Tai and if she was alone, but also anyone who might have been hanging around on the bridge, acting suspiciously."

"Shonda, can you find out who Tai's friends were and see if you can talk to any of them. Find out if they saw Tai last night or if they knew who she was with. Also, ask if they knew if Tai was in any kind of trouble, and find out what her metal state was like."

Shonda was more likely to find common ground with a bunch of college girls than Linda. Shonda looked like someone they'd want to hang out with, while Linda could be one of their mothers. They'd talk more freely with Shonda, be less prone to feel they had to hide something.

"You mean was she showing any signs of wanting to throw herself off a bridge?"

"Among other things, yes." He turned to one of his other DCs. "Linda, you're requesting phone records and take on social media, too."

"No problem, boss."

"Mallory, can you take a closer look at the parents. Apparently, the father isn't on the scene. Let's find out a bit more about him. When was the last time he was around? When did he last have contact with Tai or her mother? Does he pay regular child maintenance?"

She noted it down and nodded. "Got it."

"The mother, too," Ryan added. "She's devastated, understandably, but potentially, she's the last person to have seen her daughter alive, that we know of. We need to find out more about her and this new relationship she's having. Could she have been jealous of Tai and Richard? Jealous enough to want Tai off the scene?"

He thought he had everything covered, though he was sure further leads would unravel themselves soon enough.

Ryan clapped his hands together. "Right, let's get to work, everyone, and find out exactly what happened to Tai Moore."

Chapter Seven

Ryan grabbed lunch and ate at his desk as he worked. Despite his attitude, Bob Newton came through with the CCTV footage from the bridge, and it was passed on to Dev and Craig to work through. For the moment, they were focusing their attention on the main camera that was pointed at the area Tai went over. If they could narrow down the time she was there, they could expand the search through the rest of the footage to try and see what other people and vehicles were in the same location at that time. If they got lucky, they might be able to locate some more witnesses.

Ryan still had other cases he was wrapping up, so he needed to move his attention to those while trusting his team to work on the Tai Moore case. He was thankful he didn't have any court dates in the immediate future. He already felt like there weren't enough hours in the day and that he was being pulled in ten different directions.

It didn't take long before Dev caught his attention. "Boss, I think I've found something."

Ryan left his desk. Dev remained sitting, and Ryan drew up a chair beside him. Craig had also been going through footage, but he left his screen to wheel his seat across the floor, pushing it with his feet while still sitting in it, so he could also look over Dev's shoulder.

"As you know, I've been watching the footage from the CCTV cameras from the bridge," Dev said. "The quality is great right up until it gets dark and the fog comes in, then the cameras switch to black-and-white thermal imaging. The height of the camera from the bridge means we can easily make out the shapes of people walking across, but getting any detail of faces is tricky. As I'm sure you know, the hotter parts of the body show up whiter, with the cooler areas showing as dark grey."

"Would digital forensics be able to get anything in greater detail?" Ryan wondered.

"They can certainly try, but if the person has their head down or is wearing a hood, or even keeps their back to the camera, that's not going to be much use to us."

Ryan nodded in understanding. "Any sign of Tai yet?"

"I believe so, yes. At eleven-oh-seven, what appears to be a young woman crosses the bridge from the direction of the city and stops on the Somerset side, right where we believe Tai fell from."

Dev hit a few buttons on the keyboard and pulled up a freeze-frame of the footage he'd been talking about. Ryan frowned and leaned in closer. As Dev had described, it wasn't a great image.

"Is that Tai?" Ryan didn't want to get spun off in the wrong direction investigating the actions of a person who just happened to be in the same place, rather than someone who was actually connected to the investigation. He preferred to avoid wild goose chases.

"It is, though it's hard to make out any features."

Craig shook his head. "I don't think that's her?"

Ryan glanced over at him. "Any reason why?"

"I'm not sure. I just don't think we can say for definite that it is"

Dev's fingers tapped across the keys, making the image larger. "If you keep watching, you'll see that it definitely is."

"Okay, let's say it's Tai," Ryan said. "She's alone, right?"

"For the minute." Dev hit 'play' on the screen, and the activities of the bridge on the night Tai died continued in a strange grey-and-white world. "Several people walk right past her. At eleven-thirteen, a man and a woman pass her from the Somerset side, heading across to Clifton. We'll assume they're a couple, since they're holding hands. It's difficult to figure out their age, but from the style of clothes and the way they're walking—do you see the man has a kind of swagger—I'd say they're in their twenties."

Ryan steepled his fingers to his lips. "Good. We can do a social media appeal for anyone around that age to come forward as a possible witness. Even if they didn't notice Tai, they might have spotted someone else hanging around."

Dev continued to play the footage.

"What's she doing now?" Ryan asked.

"Think she's checking her phone."

Ryan bit his lower lip. "I agree. Which means she definitely had her phone with her on the bridge. So what happened to it? Did someone take it? Or did it go over the bridge with her and we just haven't found it yet?"

"The other thing about her checking her phone," Dev continued, "is that it makes me think she's waiting for someone. It's just what you do, isn't it? If you have to hang around for someone, you check your phone to see if you've got a message to say they'll be late or they're on their way, and you distract yourself by checking social media so you're not just standing there like an idiot."

"We've got Linda going through Tai's social media," Ryan said. "Maybe she posted something while she was waiting."

"Or perhaps commented or liked someone else's post? Keep watching."

Ryan did.

"At eleven-fifteen, someone else walks past her, this time going the other way, coming from Clifton. Looks to me to be male, wearing a suit, walking briskly. I think he might have sensed her there, as he turns in her direction. See?" Dev paused the video at the point where the white shape of the man's face turns towards where Tai was standing.

"Did he see her?" Ryan wondered.

"It's impossible to say. It was dark, which wouldn't normally be too much of a problem, as the bridge is lit, but the fog complicates things. The lights from the bridge get reflected back in the white and make it even harder to see anything."

"We're still going to need to find whoever this man is."

"Agreed. I'll send all of this over to digital forensics and see if they can make the facial images clearer. Anyway, this is where it gets interesting."

The grey-and-white shaded figure of Tai Moore vanished offscreen for a moment. Had she left? Was this when she'd jumped or was thrown? Ryan's gaze skirted across the other screens. "Does she show up on any of the other cameras?"

"No, she's out of view at this point. But keep watching."

Ryan glanced at the time again, the seconds flipping over. How long was she out of view? What was she doing in that time? Was she meeting with someone? Talking to someone on her phone? It was frustrating not being able to see.

Forty-three seconds passed before she stepped back into view. At least, he assumed it was her.

A second person appeared in the corner of the screen, coming out from beneath the tunnel that led onto the bridge. The person had their head down, though the shape of their body was clearly defined in whites and lighter greys. They stopped in front of Tai, but now they had their back to the camera.

"Can we get a better look?" Ryan asked.

Dev shook his head. "I've tried to enhance it, but between the fog and the dark, it doesn't get any clearer."

"Male? Female?"

"Impossible to say. They're of average build and height, not distinctly one way or the other."

It was true. Where the images of the previous people who'd walked past could be easily distinguished as being male or female, this person wasn't giving anything away.

Ryan realised he was making assumptions about the previous people, too. There was no reason why a woman couldn't be bigger built, with short hair and wearing a suit. Plenty of people were changing the stereotypical gender norms these days. Assuming something could send the investigation down completely the wrong track.

The main part of the bridge was built high, with security wiring across the top of the railings to prevent anyone from climbing over. Right at the start and end of the bridge, however, before the barriers where people had to flash their contactless cards from their car windows to pay the fee to get across, there was a red brick wall, low enough for someone to climb over, if that's what they decided.

The two figures stood close together, one bigger than the other. The bigger figure backed the smaller one up against the wall. Ryan couldn't tear his eyes away, his breath caught in anticipation, at what was about to unfold. He wished he could reach into the screen and yank the figure they assumed to be Tai out of the way and pull her to safety, but that was impossible.

She was already dead.

He couldn't save her, but he could find out who had killed her.

Onscreen, the white of the two different people seemed to blend together for a moment, creating one, much larger figure. And then they parted again and there was only the flash of movement as Tai's legs flipped up into the air and she fell backwards over the wall.

Ryan checked the time onscreen. Eleven-nineteen p.m.

"I think we can rule out suicide," Ryan said. "She was definitely murdered."

"Did whoever push her take her phone?" Dev wondered.

"They could have done. If Tai had it in her hand during the brief struggle, they could easily have snatched it before they pushed her. It's impossible to tell from the footage, though."

"Did it look as though she knew the person?" Craig asked.

"Again, it's hard to tell." Ryan tapped a pencil against his palm. "When she steps out of view of the camera, is that because she's talking to whoever pushed her? She's not in view for forty-three seconds. It might not sound like a lot, but it's enough time to have a conversation with someone. Watch."

Ryan took out his phone and set the timer for forty-three seconds and then placed it on his constable's desk. They waited for the timer to run down, most likely each imagining a conversation that might have taken place between Tai and her killer.

"That's longer than someone asking for directions," Ryan said. "Plus, she was a young woman in a small dress, who must have been conscious about standing around in the dark talking to strangers. If she didn't know them, wouldn't she have made an excuse and walked away?"

Craig stared at the screen. "It might have been a stranger. Most young girls are brought up to always be polite, and sometimes that social politeness is enough to get them killed."

Ryan agreed. "That's true. It did seem as though she was waiting for someone, though. When we get her phone records back, that should give us a better idea who she was in touch with." He gestured at the screen. "Go back again. Let's see what else we can spot that might help us. What about other cameras with different viewpoints. We know the time she was there now, so let's take a look at them."

Dev replayed the footage.

On another camera, a lorry drove by. It paused at the barrier, clearly finding issues with paying the fee.

"Who was the driver of the lorry?" Ryan wondered. "Did they see something? Yes, it was foggy, but that doesn't mean they didn't see this happen. Did we get the number plate?"

Dev froze the screen. "Yep, and the lorry has got the company name scrawled across the side. It's a refrigerated meat provider."

Ryan exhaled the air from his lungs. "Good. Let's find the driver and talk to them. They might have been the last person to see Tai Moore alive."

He got to his feet and raised his voice to get the attention of the rest of the room.

"As of now, we're treating the death of Tai Moore as a murder investigation. We have CCTV footage of her arriving at the Clifton Suspension Bridge at eleven-oh-seven p.m., and she was only there for twelve minutes before someone—as yet unidentified—pushed her over the wall at eleven-nineteen. Though we don't have any faces—as of yet, though that might change once digital forensics get their hands on the footage—we know that we have three potential witnesses who walk by Tai when she was waiting, possibly for the person who killed her. We also have the driver of the lorry who might also have seen something or the lorry might have had a dashcam, which could potentially give us a different view of the killer. The dark and fog doesn't help our case, but it's always worth trying.

"Because we didn't get any footage of the person who pushed her crossing the bridge, they must have come from the Somerset side. Now we have the exact time Tai was pushed"—he realised he couldn't say 'her death' as he didn't yet know if Tai had died upon impact or if she'd lain in the gorge dying for hours. He hoped for both the girl's sake, and that of her family, that her death had been quick. There was nothing more tortuous for a loved one than imagining a family member in pain, and possibly calling out for help, only for no one to come—"it'll make it easier for us to narrow down what times we need to be checking the CCTV of the surrounding roads. How did this person reach the bridge? Did they walk the whole way, or did they drive and park somewhere on this side of the bridge and walk the rest? If we can spot a car and get a registration plate, we might have our suspect."

Dev nodded. "I'll get these parts sent over to digital forensics and get to work on checking the rest of the CCTV."

"Great." He was going to need to get someone on to trying to find those possible witnesses. Even if they didn't see Tai, they might have seen whoever killed her hanging around near the entrance to the bridge. It was the sort of thing someone would dismiss but then might reevaluate with fresh eyes when they realised what the connection was.

They had a press officer who dealt with these kinds of appeals, so Ryan would delegate the search to them.

"Mallory," he said, addressing his sergeant. "Can you go and tell Tai's mother that Tai's death is now officially a murder investigation."

She rose from her desk. "I'll go right away."

It was heading into the afternoon now, and they still had a lot of work to do.

"If anyone had plans this evening," he said, "I suggest you cancel them. It's going to be a late one."

A groan went around the office, but it was good-humoured. These kind of hours were expected when a new murder investigation was launched. He'd order in some takeaway for everyone later—Chinese, Indian, pizza. Whatever they fancied. No one worked well on an empty stomach, and it was the small gestures that made a team think they were being thought of and appreciated.

Chapter Eight

Ryan ran both hands over his face, trying to rub some of the tiredness out of his eyes. It had been a long day, and he felt as though he'd spent far too much time staring at screens. It wasn't his favourite part of the job. He preferred being able to talk to people, but then he didn't think anyone liked to file reports.

He fished the front door keys to his building out of his pocket and slotted them into the lock. It was late, and half the flats' windows were in darkness.

His mind turned over the case. They'd made progress, but they didn't have any solid leads yet. The mother's boyfriend might be someone to keep an eye on, especially with his past convictions, but it turned out he had an alibi in the form of Tai's mother. That didn't mean the two of them weren't in it together, though. After all, it had looked like someone Tai knew on the CCTV footage. Ryan thought that he wanted to meet the man himself, see if he could get a feel for him. He believed he was a good judge of character and would be able to tell if he was lying or not. Besides, it would get him out of the office.

He opened the front door and stepped into the entrance hall of the block of flats. A pile of unopened mail sat on the hall console, and he picked it up and rifled through them, selecting any of the items that had his name and address on. They weren't anything interesting, just the usual bank statements and bills.

To his right, the door to the first flat opened, and a wrinkled face topped with white hair peered out.

"There you are," Mrs Furst said. "Haven't seen you come home the last couple of nights."

"Oh, that's because I haven't."

Why did he feel guilty? Like he was cheating on his eighty-year-old neighbour. He didn't want to jinx things, however. He felt like mentioning the new relationship between him and Donna would risk spoiling it.

A flush of heat went through him. He was...happy. An emotion so alien to him he almost didn't recognise it. He wanted to enjoy it, but the whole time he was just waiting for something to go wrong.

The sense of precariousness at his newfound happiness didn't do his OCD much good, but things had been much better since the death of Cole Fielding—the young man responsible for Hayley's hit-and-run—and Donna getting the all clear. Cole Fielding dying had felt like a new start for both of them. They'd never forget their daughter Hayley or what had happened to her, but now Cole was no longer walking this earth, it was as though the oxygen had been put back into the air.

Happiness was tenuous, though. He'd suffered enough in his life to know that for a fact. He saw it every day in his job, people who'd been coasting through life, taking their happiness for granted, only to have it whipped out from under them in an instant.

He wasn't completely better. He doubted he ever would be. But he was doing his best to hide his OCD from Donna. He didn't want to do anything that might ruin their newly reformed relationship.

His neighbour narrowed her small, milky-blue eyes at him from behind her glasses.

"You've got a new woman, haven't you? Or is it a man? You can never really know these days, though you don't seem the type."

"A woman," he said and then realised he'd confirmed her suspicions.

"So you do have one," she said triumphantly.

"Not a new one, no."

She threw him a wink. "Well, you dark horse. Good to see you've still got it in you."

"I'm not that old, Mrs Furst!" he protested.

She shook with laughter. "I'm just pulling your chain. You're a spring chicken compared to me. Got to make the most of it while you still can. I thought I was over it all when I was in my forties and now I look back and realise how young I still was. I wish I'd slept around a bit more."

Ryan had to stop his jaw from dropping. Heat rushed to his cheeks at the idea of his neighbour sleeping around. It wasn't a mental image he was prepared for.

He blustered his way through it. "I'm sure you still have all the men knocking down your door."

She flapped a hand. "Ooh, wouldn't that be nice. I keep reading about all this online dating—swiping left and right and all that. Sounds like fun. Maybe I should get myself on one of those apps."

"Just be careful if you do. There are predators on those apps. They might want to take advantage of you."

She threw him a wink. "I might just let them."

At his horrified expression, she chortled again and disappeared back inside her flat.

Ryan blinked and shook his head and continued to his own flat. He hoped he had half of her energy when he reached her age. She still walked three miles every day, even though it took her forever. She'd told him often enough 'use it or lose it'. He guessed that was both in the physical and mental sense of the word.

He entered the flat and closed and locked the door behind him. He hoped he was going to get some sleep tonight, though he wasn't going to put any money on it. Every time he closed his eyes, he'd have Tai Moore's dead face in his thoughts. Seventeen years old. Life was so unfair. She could have been like Mrs Furst and lived another sixty-plus years, and instead some sick bastard had decided to snuff out her life.

Ryan helped himself to a small glass of red wine. He needed sleep, but first he needed to wind down. He knew from years of experience that getting in straight from a case and attempting to sleep simply didn't work.

He wished he'd gone to Donna's instead of coming back to this soulless flat. He took out his phone and stared at the screen. Would he get away with calling her now, he wondered, or maybe even just sending her a text message? But he didn't want to disturb her if she was already asleep. She'd been through a lot recently and needed her rest. The last thing she needed was him calling her up late at night and offloading about his job.

Ryan took a sip of his wine, let out a sigh, and sank deeper into the sofa. At least he'd avoided the misery of having a microwave meal for one by eating a takeaway with his colleagues at the office. He patted his stomach, trying to tell if there was a layer more fat there than normal. He knew how easy it was to end up with a gut if he wasn't careful. The days of his twenties and thirties of being able to eat whatever he wanted were long behind him.

He watched something mindless on television while he finished his drink, deliberately ignoring the news, and hoped he'd switched his brain off enough to get some sleep.

Chapter Nine

Mallory found a place to park on her busy road. Tiredness wrapped around her like a shroud. Dealing with murders of young girls was always hard on her. No matter how much she tried to harden herself against it, she didn't think she'd ever be able to, not fully. Perhaps it made her better at her job, but it wasn't easy.

It was still very early days in the investigation. Teenage girls could be secretive. Tai might have got herself involved with someone online or maybe had an older boyfriend she'd been keeping a secret from her family and friends. Nothing ever happened within a bubble, though. No matter how much she thought she'd kept things hidden, there would be a trail the police would be able to follow.

Mallory had her head down, making sure she had her phone in her bag and hadn't left it in the car, so she didn't look up until she was almost at her front door.

"Oh!" she said. "What are you doing here?"

Daniel Williamson from Helping Hands had been sitting on her doorstep, but now he rose to standing. Daniel helped her with Oliver, because of her brother's Downs Syndrome.

"I wanted to talk to you."

"You could have phoned."

"I have phoned, and I messaged you, too, but you've been ignoring me. You've basically ghosted me."

Was it considered ghosting when you'd already told the person you didn't want to hear from them? That felt like a manipulatory tactic to her. She'd put up boundaries, and he was overstepping them by continuing to call and message her when she'd told him, face to face, that she didn't think it was a good idea for them to keep seeing each other. It made it difficult that he was still spending time with Oliver, because when she saw the missed calls from Daniel come up on her phone, she worried that it was about her brother, but after the first couple of times of calling Daniel back and realising he wanted to talk about *them* and not Ollie, she'd stopped returning the calls. Now, she called Helping Hands directly if she was worried about something.

"I'm sorry," she said, "but I've already told you that I don't think it's a good idea, us seeing each other outside of you working with Ollie. It makes things too complicated, and I don't want Ollie to be the one who gets caught in the middle."

"You're dumping me because of your brother."

"I'm hardly dumping you. We went out for dinner a couple of times."

His nostrils flared, a muscle in his jaw ticking. "It was more than that, Mallory, and you know it. I've practically been a part of the family, and you're treating me this way?"

This was exactly what she'd been worried about. She should never have allowed those boundaries to have blurred. She'd let things cool off after Ollie had told her that Daniel had been asking questions about her job that made Oliver feel uncomfortable. When she'd asked Daniel about it, he'd grown defensive, and it had been enough to make Mallory want to back off. She'd never been completely comfortable about getting involved with her brother's helper, and yes, maybe she had been frightened off at the first little blip, but it had also solidified her initial instinct that it wasn't a good idea.

In her job, she'd learned to trust her instincts and she didn't plan on stopping now.

She checked the time on her phone. "Daniel, it's almost eleven. It's been one hell of a day, and I'm exhausted. I really don't want to have this conversation now."

"Then let's have it another time. Let me take you out for a drink." He seemed to perk up, as though she'd just given him a glimpse of light.

Mallory sighed, suddenly even more exhausted than before. "That's not what I meant. I meant there's nothing to talk about. I just need you to be Oliver's helper, nothing more. I'm sorry."

She shouldn't have apologised, she realised. She was allowed to not want to see someone outside of a professional capacity. She didn't have to be sorry about it.

"I'm in your home twice a week, Mallory. I don't think it's much to ask that we have a conversation."

"I'm happy to have a conversation if it's about Oliver, but otherwise, we really don't have anything to talk about."

She didn't want to disappoint him or let him down. She was a decent person and she couldn't help feeling guilty if she'd led him on. But then she reminded herself that she was allowed to say no. Having a drink or a meal with someone didn't give them the right to expect anything more.

"I know you've been avoiding me. You make sure I'm long gone before you get home."

That was true, she had, but it was easier that way. She'd wanted to avoid exactly this sort of confrontation.

"I have a busy job, Daniel. That's the whole point of having you come in and spend time with Ollie. If I was home all the time, I wouldn't need the support from Helping Hands."

"Sounds to me like your job is just a convenient excuse to keep people at arm's length."

She let out a sigh. "Seriously, I'm shattered. I have an early start in the morning. I don't want to have this conversation. All I want is to go to bed."

"Fine, but you know I'll be back. You can't get rid of me that easily."

Her skin prickled with unease. Did he mean that to sound as threatening as it had?

For the first time, she wondered if she was going to need to ask the people at Helping Hands if they could send someone else in replacement of Daniel. It had been the exact thing she'd been hoping to avoid. Ollie got on great with Daniel, and Mallory loved that her brother had a male influence in his life who was of a similar age—or at least not too much older. She didn't think Ollie would light up in the same way as he did with Daniel if they sent someone else along.

Daniel continued to stand in the way, blocking her front door. Again, she wasn't sure if he was doing so deliberately or if it was just because he'd been waiting on the doorstep. She was primed to seeing threats everywhere and she didn't want to read danger into a situation when there wasn't any.

She kept her voice calm but firm, but flutters of nerves danced in her stomach. "I'd like to go inside now, Daniel. Can you move out of the way, please?"

He pressed his lips together and crossed his arms over his chest. The body language was unmistakably defensive, and she drew in a breath, certain she hadn't been overexaggerating the situation in her head. It was late, and dark, and there was no one else around. But then his shoulders slumped, and he moved to one side.

He still hadn't left, however. He just stood there, watching her.

Mallory forced herself to face him. "Goodnight, Daniel."

She held her ground.

He lifted his chin at her in a kind of reverse nod and then shoved his hands in his pockets and walked away. She stayed where she was until he vanished out of view, and then the energy drained from her body like someone had pulled the plug. Her hand shook as she managed to get the key into the lock and turned it. She pushed inside the house and quickly shut and locked the door behind her.

Was it the confrontation that had shaken her so much?

Daniel had always seemed like a decent bloke. She'd never have gone out with him, or let him spend time with Oliver, if she'd felt any differently. Had that changed now? Or had her reaction to him been because she was overtired and shaken up after the long day and the discovery of Tai Moore's body?

It was hard not to have violence against women at the forefront of her mind. Most women were killed by someone they knew.

She went upstairs and peeped into her brother's bedroom. He still slept with a nightlight, so she was able to make out the shape of him beneath his bedcovers.

"Oliver?" she whispered, torn between not wanting to wake him and wanting to have him to talk to. "You awake?"

He didn't so much as stir.

She backed out of the room and gently closed the door behind her. She was grateful he was sleeping again. A fire in their kitchen had disturbed both of their sleep for months afterwards, Ollie constantly having nightmares about it. It had been a rough time. Oliver was bigger and stronger than her, and when he'd been caught in one of the night terrors, he hadn't realised she was there. He'd caught her in the face with one of his fists one time, and she'd been worried that people would see the injury and declare that she wasn't coping with both her work and taking care of him.

But things had got better.

She prayed that if she had to stop Daniel from coming, it wouldn't set Oliver backwards again.

Chapter Ten

Faye woke in a strange room, completely unaware of where she was. It took her brain a few moments to click into gear, flicking through each possibility one after the other. Was she on holiday? Away on a conference? But the room she'd found herself in was nothing like the stark, impersonal spaces of the sort of hotels she was put in then.

The curtains were chintzy, covered in little pastel flowers, as was the duvet and pillow covers. Above her head, a paper ball of a lampshade hid the bare bulb, and the ceiling had the kind of stippled texture that had been popular several decades ago.

The magnitude of her situation washed over her afresh, and she curled onto her side, her hand tucked beneath her cheek, and cried silent tears. She tried not to let her shoulders shake, for fear that her daughter, lying in the bed beside her, would notice her crying. It wasn't as though she would need to explain the reason for her tears, but she was worried if Chloe asked her what was wrong, or showed her any kind of sympathy, she would lose it completely. Inside, she raged, and she feared that if she let this hold on herself go, she would snap. She imagined herself screaming and tearing at her hair, kicking at the walls, and knocking over furniture.

But she couldn't do that. She had to stay strong for her daughter, so instead, she cried quietly and did her best not to wake her.

The tears were for everything they'd lost.

She thought of her friend, Sally, who was going through a tough time at the moment after finding a lump in her breast. Sally had an appointment coming up for a biopsy, and now Faye realised she wouldn't be around to support her. Had she just given Sally another thing to worry about by vanishing?

What about her parents? Chloe's grandparents. They were going to worry. They lived down in Polzeath in Cornwall, and they only saw each other once every few months, so Faye hoped they wouldn't even notice she and Chloe had been gone for a few days, if not longer. But if the police started asking questions, they were bound to send someone to her parents' house and see if she was there, and then they would worry.

She cried for her daughter, too, and the innocence lost. She cried for the uncertainty of their future.

And, as stupid as it was, considering everything else, she cried for her lost home—the bed she snuggled into peacefully every night, the kitchen she had chosen herself, with the soft-close drawers and the white granite worksurfaces. She cried for her sofa and the television she liked to watch with a glass of chilled Sauvignon Blanc most evenings. But she realised she wasn't really upset about losing any of those things. It was her life she was crying for—how she'd had no choice but to leave it all behind. And she was crying for Chloe's future and the uncertainty that now held.

Movement came beside her, and she wiped her tears and glanced over to see Chloe still sound asleep, her hair all over her face. The teenager's long limbs took up more space than Faye, and she marvelled at how her daughter, who had once been so tiny, was now the same height as her.

Faye wished she could rewind time and take Chloe back to being that small girl who'd relied on her for everything. For so long, it had seemed to Faye that her daughter was an extension of herself, and it wasn't until Chloe was around three years old that it dawned on Faye that one day her daughter would have her own life, completely independent to her. That she would be her own person and wouldn't need her mother anymore.

But now Chloe was almost grown, and she still needed Faye, now more than ever.

Faye slipped out of bed, careful not to wake Chloe, and used the adjoining bathroom. The suite was in what could only be described as salmon pink. She wondered if the owner of the B&B was up yet. They'd met briefly the night before. Faye had been aware that she'd probably come across as rude, not wanting to stand around and chat, but she didn't want to have to lie or say anything that might make them memorable.

A small electric kettle sat on the dressing table beside a couple of mugs and a selection of teas and coffees. She was parched and so filled the kettle from the bathroom tap and set it to boil.

Chloe, disturbed by the movement, groaned and shifted.

"Morning, love," Faye said. "Fancy a coffee?"

Chloe was more of a coffee drinker than tea, something Faye put down to social media influence. Coffee was cool. Tea was for old people, like her.

"Yeah, thanks, Mum."

Faye set about emptying tiny packets of sugar and coffee into one of the mugs and peeling back the tiny foil lid of the long-life milk.

She was still trying to decide what to do about her boss. Was she better off making contact, letting him know there had been a family crisis and that she needed to take a couple of weeks due to a family emergency? Was it better to just vanish and not give any details or way for anyone to get in touch with them? Or would that cause even more problems? The last thing she wanted was for her boss or Chloe's school to contact the police. If she got in touch and said there had been a family emergency—maybe even somewhere abroad—it might buy them some time. The thing she was worried about was that if the police did start looking into them, then they'd be able to track down the IP address she'd used, or figure out what mobile tower her phone had pinged off, or some other clever thing like that, and they'd be able to find them.

Chloe sat up and pushed her hair away from her face.

"Are you hungry?" Faye asked. "The landlady said breakfast would be available between seven and nine."

"Seven and nine? Is it really that early?"

Faye glanced at the LED clock on the bedside table. "Yep. Seven twenty-five, to be exact."

"Jeez. Without my phone, I have absolutely no idea what time it is."

"You know, we were able to tell the time before mobile phones came along," Faye said, teasing her.

"By the direction of a shadow on a sundial, you mean?" Chloe teased her right back in return.

To her surprise, Faye laughed. It didn't feel like she should be laughing, considering everything that had happened, but it still felt good. She definitely didn't feel old—or even of an older generation—but she and Chloe often had this banter where Chloe acted as though her mother was completely ancient and out of touch, and Faye acted as though Chloe was completely clueless about everything in life that didn't revolve around her phone.

Would all that change now? It would if they were found. She didn't even want to think about how things would change between them then.

"So, are you hungry or not?"

Chloe pulled a face. "Not. You know I can never eat in the morning."

"We're going to have to get back on the road soon. I don't want you saying we need to stop for food as soon as we get moving again."

Breakfast had been included in the price of the room, and money was tight now. They only had what Faye had been able to draw out before they'd left. If she tried to use a cashpoint or her card anywhere, it would make it easier for someone to find her.

Chloe snuggled back into bed. "I won't."

Faye put the coffee on the bedside table and took a couple of sips of her tea. Her stomach gurgled. Even if her daughter wasn't hungry, she was, and she'd be starving soon enough. Could she leave Chloe here while she went downstairs and got something to eat? If she locked the door behind her, Chloe would be safe.

"Okay. Well, I'm going to pop down and grab some toast. I won't be long. Try to get yourself ready to leave while I'm gone. You know we can't stay in one place too long."

Faye left the room and went downstairs.

The small dining room was dotted with tables and chairs. At the far end, a longer table covered in a white tablecloth contained the breakfast offerings. Several clear tubs filled with various cereal options. A toaster with bread and crumpets beside it. Jugs with juices and tiny glasses.

She wasn't alone. A couple of builder types sat at one of the tables opposite one another, shovelling cereal into their mouths, their plates teetering with stacks of toast.

"Good morning, dear. Sleep well?"

She jumped at the landlady's voice.

She hadn't. It had felt as though she'd been awake until the sun had come up and had only then fallen into a couple of hours of restless sleep, but the landlady didn't need to know that. If she mentioned that she hadn't been able to sleep, the landlady would more than likely inquire as to why. Right now, Faye would do anything to avoid questions.

The landlady, whose name she thought was Marion, or perhaps Miriam, guided Faye to one of the spare tables.

"Can I get you some fresh tea or coffee?" she offered.

Faye conjured a smile. "Tea, please."

"Where's that beautiful daughter of yours?"

"Oh, still sleeping." She gave a small shrug. "Teenagers," she said by way of a reason.

Marion or Miriam chuckled. "Oh yes. I remember that well, though both of mine are in their thirties now. I'm hoping I'll get grandchildren one day, but they seem intent on focusing on their careers. Anyway, let me get you that drink. Tea, was it?"

"Yes, tea, thank you."

The landlady bustled off again, and Faye went to the table containing the food. She selected a couple of crumpets and some spread, then added a banana on the side of the plate. She was hungry, but in a strangely sickly way that she put down to nerves and adrenaline. She knew if she didn't eat the sensation would only get worse.

Faye took her seat and busied herself spreading butter and marmite on the hot crumpet. She wished she had her phone to distract her, missing that little burst of endorphins she got from checking in on Facebook and conversing with online friends. Even a book would have done as a distraction, making her feel less lost, but she always read on a Kindle these days and hadn't even dared take that with her in case she accidentally logged in to the Wi-Fi somewhere and they were able to use that to find her.

Movement came behind her and, nervously, she glanced over her shoulder.

A smartly dressed man in his forties walked in. His gaze landed on Faye and quickly darted away again.

Faye froze, her shoulders stiffening. She tracked the man as he made his way across the room and selected a table. He took a seat, but sat facing her, so they could see each other across the room. Now she felt like she couldn't look up in case she caught his eye, so she focused on her crumpet. But it was as though the man's gaze was a laser and she could feel it trained on her the whole time.

She was being stupid, wasn't she? It was only a man in a suit. He was probably staying here for work and had an appointment somewhere locally—sales or something like that. It was nothing to worry about—he was just a man staying at a bed and breakfast, like everyone else here—but when she glanced over again, she caught him looking once more.

They locked eyes, and her heart lurched. She sucked in air, trapping it in her lungs. It was like receiving an electric shock.

Leaving her food where it was, she shot to standing and turned to hurry from the room. She couldn't have said for sure that the man was watching her go, but she sensed the weight of his gaze on her back.

Marion's voice chased her out of the dining room. "Excuse me! You forgot your tea."

Faye didn't even bother responding. She just prayed that whoever the man was, he wasn't following her. But then perhaps he wouldn't even need to. It wasn't as though the bed and breakfast had many rooms, and their car was parked outside. If he wanted to follow her, she'd made his job easy for him.

She raced up the stairs, fumbling for the room key, and burst through the door.

"We need to go," she announced to Chloe.

Chloe was still in bed, the television remote in her hand as she flicked through the crappy selection of programmes. "What? Why?"

"There's a man downstairs. He was giving me strange vibes."

Chloe rolled her eyes. "Seriously, Mum?"

"Don't you 'seriously' me. Get up. Get dressed. We're leaving."

Maybe she was overreacting, but how could she not overreact after what had happened?

She flew around the room, grabbing their few belongings and stuffing them into their bags.

"Get a move on," she snapped.

"I am."

But it was as though someone had put the slow motion button on for Chloe, and the faster Faye moved, increasingly urgent, the more her daughter dragged her feet.

"Hurry up."

"Stop nagging."

Faye threw down the bag. "I am doing this for you, Chloe. I am doing all of this for you. I have uprooted my entire life, and left my home and job and friends behind, all for you. Because of what *you* did. I am trying to keep you safe, and all I'm asking is that you get a fucking move on."

Chloe's eyes widened at her outburst. "Okay, fine, I'm coming."

Within ten minutes, they were back in the car and leaving the B&B and the strange man behind them. While it most likely was nothing and she *had* been overreacting, Faye couldn't stop herself glancing in the rearview mirror, making sure no one was following.

Chapter Eleven

Ryan arrived back in the office that morning after not having enough sleep, despite his best efforts. He could never get his mind to stop spinning when he was right at the start of a case like this. Time sleeping always felt like time wasted, and he hated to think of Tai Moore's killer out there thinking they were going to get away with it.

Too many people thought they were smarter than the police. Ryan's aim was to make sure he proved them wrong.

He rubbed at gritty eyes and headed straight for the coffee machine. Several colleagues nodded their *hellos* and *good mornings* at him, each of them with the air of too much work and not enough sleep hanging over them.

One by one, his team filtered into the office.

Mallory headed straight to her desk, her head down, not speaking to anyone. She turned on her computer and busied herself at her desk, without even getting a drink first. She was normally happy to chat with whoever she came across.

Instinct told him something was up with her, but he couldn't make her tell him if she didn't want to. The people he worked with were allowed their privacy just as much as he was. What he didn't want was detectives who were distracted and for it to affect their work.

He carried his coffee over to her desk. "Morning. You look like you could use one of these."

She glanced up but didn't smile. Her face seemed pinched. "No, I'm fine. Were there any developments in the Tai Moore case overnight?"

She'd jumped straight in, deliberately avoiding any small talk.

"Unfortunately not, but we have a lot to get on with today."

"I thought it would be a good idea for us to speak to Tai's mother's boyfriend separately," Mallory said. "Yesterday, her mother was in too much of a mess for us to get anything valuable from her, and the boyfriend, Richard Foyle, sat holding her hand the whole time. She might not have felt she could speak freely with him right there."

"I thought the same thing last night," he admitted. "I'd like to meet the man for myself. Get a feel for him."

"Yes, I think it's worth checking out. He's younger than the mother, so there might have been some hostility between Richard and Tai. Maybe Tai felt like he was closer to her age than her mother's."

"Let's go and track him down after the morning briefing. You okay to take the lead on the interview?"

"Can do, boss."

She was already refocused on her computer.

Ryan hesitated, still picking up on the vibe that something was wrong. "Everything all right with you? Oliver okay?"

She gave a strained smile. "Yeah, Oliver's great. I'm just tired. Late night and didn't sleep well."

"You'd tell me if it was anything else?"

"Of course."

He nodded his acceptance, aware he couldn't pressure her any further. He made a mental note to keep an eye on her, though.

Ryan glanced around the office. It looked like everyone was in now, so he called that morning's briefing to ensure everyone knew what their actions were for the day. Between interviewing the numerous people Tai had had in her life, and requesting and watching hours' worth of CCTV recordings, plus going through the licence plates of every vehicle that went over the bridge during the times Tai was there, was hugely time consuming. They still needed to track down the people who'd passed her on the bridge shortly before she was killed and question them, too.

It was Ryan's job to coordinate his team to ensure all of those things were being done, but he also wanted to get out there as well. He hated to be stuck behind a computer or on the phone all day.

He went to the incident board and straightened everything so it lined up. If something was off, it caught his eye and muddled his thoughts.

Shonda stuck her head around the edge of the door. "DCI Hirst is asking to catch up with you."

He finished straightening the photographs. "Thanks, Shonda. I'll be right there."

He went to his boss' office, knocked on the door, and entered. DCI Hirst sat behind her desk. He noted a new picture frame containing a photograph of her adult daughter holding a tiny baby. DCI Hirst had become a grandmother recently, though Ryan would never have taken her for one. He didn't think of her as being too much older than him, and she certainly wasn't one for sitting around knitting booties. He even struggled to picture her reading bedtime stories, unless they involved cops and robbers, but then she'd raised her own children well enough.

"Morning, Ryan," she said. "How are things going with the Tai Moore case?"

"Slowly, so far. We've got CCTV footage of the incident, where someone has pushed her from the bridge, but the camera is a distance away, plus it's infrared. That makes it hard to make out any features. It doesn't help that the person who pushed her had their back to the camera."

"Do you think they knew the camera was there?"

"I'd say so. They're visible up on the wall, though the fog might have obscured them. I believe Tai was there to meet someone. Was it the same person who killed her? We're not sure yet. She stepped into a blind spot beneath the tunnel, and maybe that's where her killer had planned to attack her, but then she moved back out in view of the camera. Maybe the killer felt they were left with no choice but to do what they did, even if it meant getting caught on camera."

DCI Hirst propped her chin on her knuckles. "You think she spoke to the person when she was out of shot?"

"She was offscreen for forty-three seconds, so yes, I'd say so. We still haven't found her phone, so either it fell with her or the killer took it. If they took it, that might be because there's incriminating evidence on it. I've requested phone records, and the mother has handed over the girl's laptop for digital forensics."

Ryan filled her in on the potential witnesses as well, plus the setup with the mother's boyfriend.

"As you can see, we've got a lot of work to do."

She waved him out of the office. "Don't let me keep you then."

Ryan called his team together to make sure they were all on the same page.

"Have we got hold of the lorry driver who was on the bridge shortly before Tai was pushed?" he asked.

Craig spoke up. "The delivery company passed on the driver's mobile number, and I was able to speak to him over the phone. He says he didn't see anything, though. Was more focused on getting through the barriers with all the fog than what was around him. He didn't have a dashcam."

"Damn. What about all the other vehicles that were caught at that time?"

"I'm working through them, but so far, no one saw anything. The fog was so thick, it must have hidden Tai from the view of any drivers, and like the lorry driver said, they were more focused on not hitting anything than anyone who might have been standing on the bridge."

"We've got more CCTV in, too," Dev said. "Street camera footage from around both the bridge and Tai's home. It's going to take some time to go through it all."

"Okay. Keep working on that. Hopefully, it'll give us a new lead." Ryan moved on, turning his attention to Linda. "Have we got anything back from her phone company yet?"

"Yes, I've got the records. She made and received several calls the day she died, plus sent and received a number of messages. I'm going through them all now."

"Good." He focused on Shonda. "Have you been able to talk to any of Tai's friends?"

"I've spoken to several of the students who classed themselves as Tai's friends, though you know what it's like with that age group when someone dies. It's like they all decide they're the dead girl's best friend. I asked to see selfies of them together to sort the attention-seekers from those who really knew her. I figured anyone who was really her friend would have photos of them together on their phone."

"Good thinking," Ryan said.

"Anyway, it seems Tai Moore was a bit of a queen bee."

Ryan arched an eyebrow. "A queen bee?"

"Yeah, she ruled the roost. She was the one who people wanted to be friends with, the one who always wore the right clothes, had the perfect makeup. The one all the other girls wanted to be like and who all the guys wanted to date, though apparently she wouldn't have touched any of them. She was untouchable by college-aged boys, saw herself as being above them."

"Did any of them mention her being into anything she shouldn't have been?"

"Not yet, but I'm still digging. I've got the feeling that while they were happy to talk about her, they also didn't want to speak ill of the dead. I'm trying to build a bit of a relationship with a couple of them, get them to trust me."

"Okay, keep me updated about how that goes. Mallory and I are going to speak to Richard Foyle today, see if there's anything suspicious with the relationship between him and Tai that we need to pay attention to."

READY TO GO?" HE ASKED Mallory when the briefing was over.

She grabbed her jacket. "Absolutely."

"We'll take my car."

Twenty minutes later, they arrived at Tai's house in Brislington. Numerous bunches of flowers were on the doorstep, a couple of cards propped next to them. Someone clearly wanted to offer their condolences but hadn't wanted to disturb them.

Ryan left them where they were and rang the bell.

Movement came from inside, and then Lorraine Moore, Tai's mother, opened the door. The poor woman looked utterly defeated, slumped and lifeless, her eyes hollowed with shadows, the whites bloodshot.

Ryan held up his ID. "Sorry to disturb you, Miss Moore. We wondered if we could have a chat with Richard?"

"He's gone into work."

That surprised him. "He went into work?" Surely Richard's job would have let him have time off, considering the circumstances.

Lorraine sniffed. "Yes, he thought it would be best to keep busy."

"What about you?"

"How can I do anything? I can barely think straight." She began to cry, covering her face with her hands.

That wasn't what he'd meant. He'd meant that Richard should have put Lorraine's needs before his own. But there was no point in getting into that with Lorraine.

"Can we have the address of his place of work?" he asked.

She sniffed and wiped her eyes. "It's the garage down on the Westpoint Industrial estate."

"Thanks."

They left her in peace and got back in the car, Ryan sliding behind the wheel. The industrial estate was another fifteen-to twenty-minute drive via Crews Hole Road.

"Seems a bit heartless to leave her alone in that state and go into work," Mallory said from the passenger seat.

Ryan was glad she'd thought the same, but he decided to play devil's advocate.

"Maybe he didn't have any choice. He might have a hard-arse as a boss. It's not as though the two of them are married."

She threw out a hand. "But they are living together. In this day and age, I'd say that made them partners."

Ryan kept his eyes on the road as he navigated the traffic. "It might be his boss who doesn't see any reason for him to get time off."

"Or the boyfriend is the one who is the hard-arse and decided he'd rather be at work than having to deal with a grief-stricken woman."

"I guess we're going to find out."

They arrived at the garage. There was a large parking area outside, filled with numerous different vehicles. The industrial smells of hot metal and petrol and the noise of grinding filled the air. A radio played somewhere in the background.

A man with a heavy gut approached, wiping oily hands on a cloth. They'd been spotted.

"Help you?" he called out to them.

Ryan held up his ID. "We're looking for Richard Foyle."

"He's just out delivering a car. He'll be back soon. You here about that poor girl's death?"

Ryan didn't answer the question. "Are you his boss?"

"That's right. I own this place. Carl Holden." He went to offer his hand but must have seen it was still smeared with oil and pulled it back again.

"I was surprised that Richard came into work today," Ryan commented.

Carl frowned. "Yeah, me, too. I did offer for him to take the day off, but he said there wasn't anything he could do at home."

"You mean you didn't tell him he had to come into work?" Mallory said.

"No!" Carl exclaimed. "I'm not that much of a prick. No matter what people might say about me. I mean, Jesus Christ, that poor girl is dead. What was she? Sixteen...seventeen years old?" He sucked air over his teeth and shook his head. "It's far too young, isn't it?"

Ryan exchanged a glance with Mallory. So, Richard had chosen to come into work today. That spoke of two things. Either he wanted to distract himself from everything that had happened or else he simply didn't care that Tai was dead.

The loud grumble of a large engine approached the garage, and they all glanced around as a sizeable truck with a car-carrying trailer on the back drove into the parking area.

A youngish man with short, light-brown hair sat hunched behind the wheel. He spotted the two detectives, and his eyes narrowed.

Carl said, "See, I told you he wouldn't be long."

Richard climbed down from the truck and stood with his hands on his hips. "What's all this about then?"

"I thought you might have been able to guess that much," Ryan said, unable to help the slightly sarcastic tone entering his voice. "We need to talk to you about Tia."

"I spoke to you lot yesterday at the house," Richard said. "I don't see why I have to go over everything again."

"I'm afraid that when a young girl has been murdered, and we don't yet know the reason behind her death, we will expect you to go over this as many times as needed. Now, is there somewhere private we can talk, or would you prefer we did this in front of your boss?"

Carl stepped backwards and jerked his chin. "You're welcome to use my office. Take as much time as you need."

Richard scowled but led them in to the building, where they crossed the garage floor to the back. A couple of offices and a possible storeroom made up the rear of the building. Richard opened the door to one of them and led them in.

On the wall hung a calendar for the previous year, the picture of an old classic car. A coffee cup with the dried remnants of a drink sat in the middle of the desk. A plant, yellow and almost unrecognisable, died in a pot on the floor.

Richard moved behind the desk and took a seat in what Ryan assumed was his boss' chair. Ryan and Mallory slid into the cheap plastic chairs opposite.

As they'd initially planned, Mallory took charge of the interview.

"I'm going to record this interview," she said, placing a small, handheld recorder on the desk between them. "I assume that'll be all right?"

Richard didn't really have much of a choice. If he caused a fuss, they'd only take him down to the station for a more formal interview. As of yet, he wasn't a suspect. Their colleagues who'd spoken to the family the previous day had already confirmed that Richard had been home with Tai's mother at the time of the girl's death. That didn't eradicate the possibility that he had someone else involved, or perhaps that Tai's mother had been lying to protect him, but right now, there was nothing directly pointing their suspicions in his direction.

There was always the possibility of that changing.

Mallory ran him through the usual routine of getting him to say his name, date of birth, and address, and then read him his rights. She got started on her first line of questioning.

"You said you were home with Tai's mother last night," she said. "Was that all night?"

"Yes, of course it was. I didn't sneak out in the middle of the night to murder my stepdaughter, if that's what you're implying." He was clearly defensive.

Mallory continued. "She's not actually your stepdaughter, though, is she? You and her mother aren't actually married."

Richard shifted in his seat. "Well, no. We're not, but she feels like my stepdaughter. That's the kind of relationship we had."

Mallory seemed surprised. "Even though you're only a few years older than Tai? Isn't it right that there's the same age difference between you and Tai as there is with Tai's mother?"

His jaw clenched. "I'm more than a few years older. I'm practically a whole generation older."

"And what was your relationship like with Tai?"

"It was fine. We got on fine."

She raised an eyebrow. "Just fine? I find it hard to believe that a teenager living in a house where her mother has brought home a younger man to move in would just be fine. You're saying there were no disagreements? No arguments?"

His gaze slipped away from her, and he pursed his lips. "I suppose there were some, now you mention it. It was all the usual stuff, though. Tai missing curfews, or coming home drunk, or staying up half the night on her phone. Obviously, she didn't appreciate me getting involved when her and her mother were fighting, but sometimes that girl could get really vicious with her tongue, and I couldn't just stand by and listen to her talk to her mother like that."

Mallory offered him a smile of sympathy. "That must have been difficult. Teenagers can be hard to live with."

Ryan thought it was good that she was making out like she understood what Richard was going through, as though she was on his side. People were more likely to open up if they felt someone understood them. It wasn't easy when dealing with someone whose chip on their shoulder was as big as Richard's.

Ryan wondered what Tai's mother saw in him. Was it just that he was younger and she'd been a single mother and had needed help and company? Had he just seen her as someone who could provide a steady home and regular meals? Or did they have a true connection and Ryan was judging them too harshly?

"People in general can be hard to live with," Richard continued, "but yeah, Tai wasn't always easy. She was just a normal teenager, though. She wanted to be independent, but obviously she wasn't old enough yet, so she acted out."

"Did she ever talk to you about problems she was having? Boy issues or stress at school?"

His line of sight drifted down to the desk. "Nah, she wouldn't talk to me about stuff like that. I'm not sure she'd even talk to her mum, to be honest."

"So what sort of things did the two of you talk about?"

He shrugged. "Easy stuff. Music. Netflix."

"What kind of things was she into?"

"Young rap artists I've never heard of, mostly, and she liked to watch these weird anime shows."

"Sounds like she was a bit of an individual."

"I don't know. Don't all the teenagers watch and listen to that sort of stuff these days?"

He shot a look over to Ryan. Ryan just grimaced and shrugged. Truthfully, he had zero idea what teenage girls liked to do.

Mallory continued. "When was the last time you saw Tai?"

"Before she went to college that morning."

"You didn't see her the evening she died?

"No. She went out about seven, and I hadn't got back yet."

Mallory angled her head. "Got back? I thought you were with Tai's mother all evening?"

"I was, during the evening, but I went out for a couple of beers after work, so I didn't get home until after she'd already left."

Ryan noted that down. They'd need to check out that alibi.

"Which pub did you go to?" Mallory asked.

He jerked his head. "The Black Horse, just down the road from here. The landlady knows me in there. She'll vouch for me."

"What time did you leave the pub?"

"About seven-thirty."

"And what time did you get home?"

"Just after eight."

"You went straight home?" she checked.

His shoulders stiffened. "Yes, I did. What are you saying? "

Ryan stepped in. "We just have to make sure we understand the bigger picture surrounding Tai and her final hours. For all we know, this could have happened because someone has a vendetta against you."

"Me?" Richard blinked. "Why would someone have a vendetta against me?"

"You have a drug charge on your record, is that right?"

Richard's jaw dropped. "From years ago. I was twenty-two and stupid!"

"But you were found with quite a large amount of cocaine on you at the time."

"I picked some up for my mates. That was all. I wasn't dealing, no matter what the courts said."

"It was enough for you to serve time," Ryan said.

"I got eight years and served four. Was let out on good behaviour. I turned my life around since then. I'm not the same person I was in my early twenties. I'm settled now and I don't go anywhere near drugs."

"What about Tai?" Ryan asked. "Do you know if she was involved with drugs or anything like that?"

"Not to my knowledge, but like I said, she didn't talk to me about stuff like that."

"Sure, but you understand why we need to ask these questions. If you were to still be dealing, and you upset the wrong people and they decided to take it out on Tai, that's something we would need to know about."

He shook his head. "You're barking up the wrong tree, mate. How about you stop wasting all of our time and go and find who actually killed her, yeah?"

Ryan leaned forwards and put his forearms on the table. "You don't seem particularly upset about Tai's death. Why did you come in to work today? Your boss said you could have had the day off. Don't you think your time would have been better spent supporting Tai's mother?"

"Maybe, but I had to get out of there. Honestly, I can't handle all that crying. That wasn't what I signed up for."

Ryan remembered Donna's ex saying something very similar when she'd got her cancer diagnosis. What the fuck was wrong with them? They thought women were just there to keep their beds warm and cook their meals and do their laundry, and the moment it looked like they'd need to offer some support in return, they couldn't get away quickly enough.

"Unfortunately, you don't always get what you signed up for in life, Richard. You just have to learn to live with it."

It wasn't Ryan's job to give people relationship advice. It wasn't as though he'd ever been any good at it himself. He knew he'd pushed Donna away after their daughter had died, and he could hardly tell this man—a stranger—that he needed to be there for his partner more. Maybe Tai's mother would be better off without him.

Richard shrugged. "Yeah, well, you also get to make choices, and if you don't like where your life is going, you can always do something to change things."

It looked as though Tai's mother was going to end up even more alone in the very near future. Ryan's heart went out to the poor woman.

Mallory slid a card across the desk. "I think that's everything, for now. I'm sure I don't need to tell you not to decide to take any trips abroad anytime soon. There's a good chance we'll need to speak to you again, and if there is anything you think of that you haven't already told us, please, do get in touch."

Richard nodded, but he didn't pick up the card.

Ryan cleared his throat and got to his feet, and his sergeant followed. He led them both out of the door and through the garage. The owner, Carl, was talking to a customer, but he spotted Ryan and Mallory leaving and lifted his hand in a wave. Ryan nodded in return.

They exited the building and went back to the car.

"What do you think?" Mallory asked, pausing at the passenger door.

"I think he's a bit of an arsehole. Did he kill Tai? I don't think so, but I'm not taking him off the table just yet. Let's get down to the Black Horse, ask around about him and check out his alibi. If he's still dealing or has those connections, I bet someone down there will know about it."

"You think anyone is going to talk to us?"

"We'll have to see. I'm guessing that'll depend on how well-liked he actually is down there."

Ryan was aware this was a job for one of the detective constables, but since they were right around the corner, he figured they might as well go and get it over and done with.

He got behind the wheel and started the engine, and drove in the direction of the pub.

Chapter Twelve

The Black Horse was a typical local boozer.

Sitting on the corner of a junction, it had a couple of wonky-looking picnic tables out the front. From the multitude of discarded cigarette butts on the pavement underneath them, and the glass candle holders that had being turned into ashtrays, it was clear this was the smokers' area. In the windows, a couple of tired flower boxes sat in the grubby frames, and paint peeled from the front door that was propped open by a four-litre water bottle filled with sand.

"Clearly nothing but the best for this place," Ryan commented, raising an eyebrow.

Mallory laughed.

It was still early, but the place was open. A television showing sport's news was on in the corner, and amazingly, an older gentleman sat on a table in front of it, already nursing a pint. There was no sign of the barman.

Ryan went to the bar. "Hello?"

The older man at the table turned around. "She's just gone down to the cellar to change a barrel. Shouldn't be a minute."

"Right, thanks,"

He narrowed his eyes. "You two coppers?"

"Detectives." Ryan showed him his ID. "We're asking around about Richard Foyle."

He sniffed. "Oh, yeah. What's he done now?"

"Nothing, we hope. His partner's daughter was killed, and we're investigating her death. We just need to make sure everyone was where they say they were at the time."

He sniffed. "You're in the right place then. Richard's always in the pub."

Ryan didn't think the man could say much when it wasn't even lunchtime yet, and he was here already, nursing a pint.

"You're not giving me the impression that you think much of Richard."

He shrugged. "There's not much to think about him. He goes to work, drinks at the pub, watches the footie."

"Do you know he has a past?"

"Yeah, everyone round here knows that. Served time, didn't he, a few years back? I was surprised when he shacked up with his missus and her daughter. Never thought the family life would be something for him, especially not when she already had a kid."

"That was out of character?"

"Oh, aye. Not sure he's ever even had a serious relationship before. But then you know what they say about not being able to choose who you fall in love with."

"I'm sorry," Ryan said, "but I didn't catch your name."

"It's Graham. Graham Clever."

"Nice to meet you, Graham. Did Richard ever mention, Tai, the daughter?"

"Not really. Didn't mention either of them, except to say stuff like 'got to be home, the missus is expecting me.'"

"And did you see him in here last night?" Ryan asked.

Graham nodded. "Yeah, until about seven-thirty, I think, but I wasn't really paying much attention to the time."

"Was he acting any differently? Did he seem anxious or more uptight than usual?"

"Nope. He had a couple of pints and left, just like normal. Nothing to make me think anything was wrong. You don't think he had something to do with that girl's death, do you? He can be a bit of a miserable prick, but I can't imagine he'd do something like that."

Ryan avoided the question. "Since you know about his past, have you seen any signs that he might still be involved in it, somehow?"

Graham widened his eyes and lifted his bushy white eyebrows. "What? With the drugs and stuff? I don't think so."

"He didn't meet anyone here you didn't know? You never saw him passing anything on to other people or anything like that?"

"Nah, but then I keep myself to myself. I wouldn't pay any attention to things like that."

A female voice called over from the bar. "These two people bothering you, Graham?"

The landlady was back from switching the barrels.

Graham flapped a hand. "Nah, they're all right, Margie. Just asking some questions about Richard Foyle."

Ryan slid one of his cards onto the pub table and tapped it. "So you've got my number, should you think of anything else."

He turned to the landlady. "Margie, is it? Can I call you that? I'm DI Chase, and this is DS Lawson. Have you got a moment to answer a couple of questions about one of your regulars, Richard Foyle?"

She was in her sixties and had a gaze hard enough to cut diamond on. "I suppose so, as long as you don't keep me too long. I'm busy."

Old Graham was literally the only customer she had, but Ryan wasn't going to point that out.

"Were you working last night?" he asked.

"Work every night, love. This place is my livelihood and my social life all rolled into one. Lucky me, huh?"

"Do you remember Richard Foyle coming in here."

"Yep. He comes in most days after work for a couple of pints before he goes home."

"What time did he leave yesterday?"

"Same as normal. Sometime after seven, I believe."

"Has he ever given you cause for concern that he might still be involved with drugs?"

She snorted in derision. "You think I'm going to tell you if I've seen drugs being passed around on my premises? What do you think I am? An idiot?"

"We're not interested in the drugs," Mallory said. "We're just trying to find out if they might have been the reason a young girl was killed last night."

Margie folded her arms across her portly chest. "Look, I feel bad for the girl and everything, but it's nothing to do with me or my pub."

Ryan glanced up at the security cameras positioned either side of the bar. "Are those cameras working?"

"Fat chance. They're just for show. Can't remember the last time they worked."

That was a pity. If they'd been able to get Richard on camera, they could have seen who he was with and judge his behaviour for themselves.

"Okay, thanks for your time," Ryan said.

He gave her a card as well, but she didn't pick it up.

He and Mallory left the boozer, grateful to be stepping out into the fresh air. They headed back to the car.

"I guess Richard was telling the truth when he told us where he was last night," Mallory said. "Unless the mother is covering for him. If he left here around seven-thirty, that would have been after the time Tai left home. Maybe the two of them banged into each other on the way. Or maybe he saw her and followed her?"

Ryan shook his head. "But why would Tai's mother cover for him?"

"Who knows. People do all sorts of things out of some kind of warped love or loyalty. He could have fed her a pack of lies about where it was. Maybe she can't bring herself to believe he's capable of hurting her daughter but also doesn't want to get him in trouble."

"Let's see what street cameras are around this area and try to follow his route home. With any luck, we might catch Tai on them, too."

Chapter Thirteen

As Mallory was about to climb into the passenger side, her phone rang in the inside pocket of her suit jacket. She quickly slipped it out and checked it.

Oliver's name came up on the screen.

"I'm sorry," she told Ryan, who was already in the car, "I'm going to have to take this."

She took a couple of steps away from the vehicle to give herself the illusion of privacy and answered the call. "Hi, Ollie. Is everything all right?"

Though her brother lived with her, he was very independent. He had a job and friends and went to various clubs—there were times where she joked he had more of a social life than she did. But ever since the fire, she'd found her heart and stomach lurching when he called her unexpectantly, a part of her always primed for there being some disaster again. The weeks and months following the fire had been so hard, and there had been moments where she'd wondered if she was still capable of living with Ollie, but they'd pushed through it. The worst part had been her fear for Oliver's future and him losing that independence, but it had all worked out in the end. She was still fearful of something happening that would put him back to that place again, however.

Ollie's voice came down the line. "Daniel didn't come today."

Her heart sank. "He didn't? That's a shame."

She hadn't received a call from Helping Hands, to say Daniel had called in sick or anything and so wouldn't make it. Normally, if he hadn't been able to get to them for whatever reason, the company would let her know, and, if possible, send someone else in his place.

She knew what was going on. Daniel was punishing her by not showing up.

"I was looking forward to seeing him."

She kept her voice bright. "Oh, well. Not to worry. Are you okay?"

"He was going to help me finish my puzzle."

"That's annoying. I'm sure you can finish it yourself, though."

"I wanted Daniel to help. It's more fun when Daniel is here."

She could hear the pout in Oliver's tone. Ollie could be insanely stubborn when he wanted, and he saw the world in black and white. In his mind, if someone said they were going to be somewhere, then they should be there.

"I know. How about I help you when I get home."

"Are you going to be late?" Now there was hope in his voice.

"I'll try not to be," she said, already experiencing a twinge of guilt.

She couldn't make any promises. This was a big case, and if something happened that meant she had to stay, then she'd have to stay. She'd have to call their parents and see if they could stop by and help him. She knew Ollie wouldn't think that was anywhere near as much fun as having Daniel or even her there, but it would have to do.

She ended the call, and anger and irritation at Daniel's behaviour rose inside her.

She needed to trust her gut instinct more. She'd always known that this would happen if things got weird between her and Daniel. She should have always kept things professional. It was her own fault really. She knew better. Now Ollie was the one who'd pay for her bad judgement.

Mallory glanced over at her boss, still sitting in the car, aware she was keeping him waiting, but he looked to be on his phone, too, so she took a couple of extra minutes.

A few swipes on her phone brought up the number for Helping Hands. She'd considered calling Daniel directly and telling him exactly what she thought of his behaviour but decided she needed to keep things professional. Letting it get personal was where she'd gone wrong in the first place.

She clamped the phone between her shoulder and ear as it rang.

"Helping Hands," a chirpy feminine voice answered. "You're speaking to Brenda. How can I help?"

"Hi, Brenda. This is Mallory Lawson, I'm Oliver Lawson's sister."

"Oh, yes, Mallory. How are you? How's Ollie doing?"

"He's doing well, thanks, but Daniel Williamson didn't show up today."

"Really? That's unusual. Are you sure you didn't get the time slots wrong?"

Mallory bit down on her frustration. "Yes, I'm sure. It's been the same for months now."

"Did you try Daniel's number directly? Maybe he's got caught in traffic."

"I'd rather not, if that's okay, Brenda. In fact, I'd prefer to schedule future visits with another one of your helpers, too, if that's all right."

There was a pause on the end of the line. "Oh, right. Has there been a problem?"

"Aside from him not showing up? No, there hasn't been, but I'd prefer to move forward with someone else."

Despite his behaviour, she didn't want to get Daniel in trouble with his place of work. She blamed herself as much as him for how things had gone down. She wouldn't make the same mistake again.

"We might need to rearrange some different times with you. I'm afraid I'm not going to be able to do that today."

"That's okay. We can manage until you find someone else suitable and work out a different schedule."

"I apologise once again for the no-show today."

"Not your fault," she said and ended the call

Ollie wasn't going to be happy about Daniel not coming anymore. She experienced a fresh pang of guilt. Bloody Daniel. Why couldn't he have just accepted her decision and carried on as normal? It wasn't as though they'd have to see each other all the time—the whole point of him coming was that he filled in some of the many, many hours she spent at work so Oliver was on his own.

But then she thought of how uncomfortable he'd made her feel standing on her doorstep last night. Maybe it was for the best that he no longer had access to her home and personal belongings.

He wouldn't have gone through any of them while she wasn't there, would he? The horrible thought of him poking through her knicker drawer while Ollie was in the bathroom, or rifling through her desk for personal letters, went through her. She chewed the quick on her thumbnail and tried to quell her rising anxiety.

No, she was overreacting. Nothing he'd done had made her think he was that kind of person. He was just a bit put out because of her rejection, that was all. It didn't make him a bad person. Before now, she'd thought he was great, hadn't she? She would never have left him in Ollie's company if she'd felt any different.

Mallory took a breath and went back to the car.

"Everything okay?" Ryan asked as she climbed in the passenger seat.

"Yes, fine. Just a mix-up with Oliver's home help."

"Is he okay?"

"Yes, he's just put out he doesn't have anyone to finish his puzzle with."

Ryan laughed. "Sounds about right. You want to grab something to eat on the way back into the office?"

She forced a smile. "Sounds good."

Ryan got the car back on the road, and Mallory stared out of the passenger window as he drove, lost in thought. She should be going over the case in her mind, but instead she worried what Daniel's reaction was going to be when he discovered that she'd requested for him to be replaced. He must have realised that was going to be the next step, however. He was the one who hadn't shown up when he was supposed to. He'd done that deliberately, knowing he would get a reaction out of her. Perhaps he thought that reaction would be her phoning him and by that way opening up line of communication rather than her contacting Helping Hands directly and requesting that he be replaced.

Her stomach churned. She hoped she hadn't just made a huge mistake.

She did her best to shrug that thought off. If she'd phoned him, she would have given him exactly what he wanted, and she wasn't about to start allowing herself to be manipulated by a man.

Chapter Fourteen

Before they reached the office, Ryan got a call from Nikki Francis to say she was ready for him, whenever he had time to pay her a visit. Since they were on the road anyway, it made sense for them to take a detour.

He and Mallory grabbed a sandwich from one of the supermarket garages. His sergeant had gone quiet again since receiving the phone call, and it was clear she was worried about Ollie.

Balancing their jobs with a homelife was never easy, and he knew she'd been relying on that company to help out. He hoped it wasn't going to cause any issues for her, because he really needed her mind on the job right now.

They ate in the car and then continued on to the mortuary.

After signing in with the woman on reception, they followed the corridors down to the examination room.

The mortuary was always a strange place to be. People spoke in muted tones, a sense of solemnity hanging over them. As they walked, their shoes squeaked against linoleum flooring. The scent of cleaning fluid and chemicals hung in the air. It wasn't unpleasant, as such, but distinctive. It was still preferable to standing over a body in the middle of a post-mortem, however, especially if the person had been dead for some time. He could handle it for a short while—in his time on the job, he'd been around smells even worse than a week-old corpse—but he was always glad to escape it.

He bet plenty of people would have thought a trip to the morgue would have set his OCD off, but the place always felt far cleaner and more sanitary than, say, a visit to the supermarket. But then it had never really been the idea of germs and dirt that had plagued him. For Ryan it had always been linked more to security and a lack of control. He was fully aware that it was losing his daughter that had sent him spiralling. He'd always had a touch of OCD, even growing up, and more so as a teenager, but they'd felt more like quirks than anything else. The compulsion to count things to ward off bad luck, or check his bag for his school things multiple times before he left the house, had been there as a teenager, but as he'd grown older, they'd faded into the background. It was just something he did—it hadn't got to a point of it being a problem.

All that had changed after Hayley died.

Nikki Francis stood outside the door of the examination room waiting for them.

"Hi, Ryan," she greeted them. "Hi, Mallory. Thanks for coming so quickly."

"We weren't far away," he said. "I hope you've got something useful to tell me."

"It's your job to be the judge of that, I'm afraid. I'll give you what information I have, you figure out if it's important or not."

She was already clothed in protective outerwear, but she took a couple of sets from the metal shelves beside her and handed them over to Ryan and Mallory. They both pulled them on, and then Nikki led them into the examination room where the body of Tai Moore lay on a metal gurney.

A post-mortem was a brutal thing—there was no getting around it. The chest and stomach cavity opened, the organs all removed, examined, and weighed. The skull opened and brain studied for signs of bruising or other trauma.

Nikki started with the basics, running through the victim's name, age, height, and weight, and then continued.

"I did a CT scan to identify any microfractures, shrapnel, or air embolisms. Because of the way she died, the number of fractures are plentiful, and they're consistent with a fall from a great height. She has a fracture of both her thoracic and lumber spine, at the thoracolumbar junction. She has fractured both legs, the right ankle joint, and the calcaneus, or as you'd more likely know it, the heel bone. She also has fractures in the upper limbs, too, both the distal radius and the elbow."

"That seems like a lot of breaks," Ryan commented.

Nikki glanced up at him. "She fell a good distance, by the look of it."

Ryan thought back to when he'd leaned over the bridge and taken in the drop below. "She certainly did. What about head injuries?"

"She had a traumatic subarachnoid haemorrhage, which is a bleed in the space around the brain. It's what I believe to be her cause of death."

"How long after she hit the ground did she die?"

Nikki shook her head. "I wish I could say instantly, but the amount of bruising that's formed after the fall makes me believe she was alive for a short time after she fell."

"Poor girl," Mallory said.

Ryan hoped Tai hadn't been conscious while she'd been lying there, dying. He didn't even want to think about the kind of pain Tai would have been in.

Nikki moved on. "I used ultraviolet light and luminol to image for bodily fluids, such as blood spatter and seminal fluid."

"And?" Ryan prompted.

"There's no sign of seminal fluid on the body, and the only blood spatter is her own."

"So she wasn't sexually assaulted?"

"I don't believe so, no."

"That'll be a relief for the family, at least."

While no one wanted to hear that a loved one had been sexually assaulted, one thing sexual assault did was leave a wealth of information as far as DNA went. Only the most careful of attackers was able to assault someone without leaving their DNA behind.

Nikki must have followed his train of thought.

"The most common places we find the DNA of an attacker on a victim is beneath the nails when they fought back, or we often find the suspect's hair strands caught between the victim's teeth. There's none here, unfortunately."

"She might have known her attacker then." Ryan thought back to the CCTV footage and how it appeared as though Tai had gone to speak to them for a short while. "Maybe she trusted them?"

"Possibly. Or it all just happened too fast for her to react."

"Or both," Ryan said. "We know from the CCTV footage on the bridge that it happened fast. The cameras are infrared, so they were able to pick up the shapes of Tai and her attacker, even though it was dark and foggy. Unfortunately, her attacker kept their back to the camera, so we can't get anything other than an estimate of their height and body weight. It's near impossible to even tell if they're male or female, though chances are they're going to be male if they were strong enough to throw her like that."

Nikki looked back to the girl's body. "I'm not sure. At five feet two inches, and only weighing forty-two kilograms, she was on the lower centile, according to her body mass index. She would have been pretty easy to throw by someone bigger."

Ryan frowned. "Is her low body weight something we should consider in our investigation? Are there any signs of issues with food? What about drug or alcohol use? Were you able to run a tox screen?"

"The tox screen came back clean. She didn't have drugs or alcohol in her system when she died. I don't believe she had any issues with food either. I checked her teeth, hair, and nails, and she seems to have been healthy. She's not underweight as such, not unhealthily so, she's just slim."

"Which would have made it easier for someone to throw her off the bridge."

"Exactly. Plus she had a last meal in her stomach."

"Any idea what she ate?"

"I'd say it was burger and chips."

He perked up. "From a takeaway?"

If Tai had visited a restaurant the night she'd died, she might have been with someone. At the very least, she might have been caught on camera at a certain time, so they'd be able to trace what route she'd taken when she'd left. Someone might have been following her. Even her interaction with whoever served her could be important. Was she frightened? Relaxed? Nervous? These little details might not seem important, but each part was like a piece of a jigsaw puzzle, allowing him to put together a picture of who Tai had been and what she'd been up to in the final hours of her life. Then he hoped that picture would form a great big arrow that pointed directly at whoever had killed her.

"It's hard to say right now. I'll send it away for analysis, but I suggest asking the family and friends where she liked to eat. That's likely to give you a better idea."

He nodded. "Good thinking, thanks."

"There's one area that interests me," Nikki said, "and that's the bruising around both her biceps. I can't say for sure, since there is so much soft tissue damage, but to me that looks like finger marks."

Ryan leaned in to get a closer look. She was right, the bruises were in the shapes of finger marks. "It was where her killer grabbed her to throw her."

"There's something else," Nikki said. "I was able to remove a few grains of pollen from her skin, above the bruising."

"Pollen? Could that have just come from vegetation around the gorge?"

She nodded. "It's possible. I'll have to send it off to a forensic botanist, see if they can match it. If it's from a tree or bush that's near where she fell, then it most likely just came from there."

"Okay, thanks. Anything else you can tell us? We know she was alive when she fell, but was her body moved at all?"

"As you know, liver mortis gives us a good idea as to whether or not a body has been moved. Once the heart stops, blood is subjected to gravity, and we see a purplish-red line forming as the blood turns to the consistency of a black gel. If the body has been moved or tampered with, there tends to be two liver mortis lines. Our victim only has one."

"We know she was alive when she fell from the bridge. We have CCTV footage of it happening. It's good to know that whoever killed her didn't then climb down and try to move or tamper with the body."

Had they climbed down to find and take Tai's phone, though? Or had they already snatched it on the bridge? Or did they not have her phone at all and it was still lying hidden between some rocks or at the bottom of the River Avon?

Nikki finished taking them through the remainder of the post-mortem, but there was little else that would help them with their case. It was frustrating, not having found any DNA from the killer. The best lead they had was the information about the final meal she'd eaten. It might help them figure out Tai's final movements and if she was with anyone.

Chapter Fifteen

As they headed back to the car, Ryan's phone rang, and Donna's name appeared onscreen.

Sorry, he mouthed at Mallory, and she nodded her understanding.

Ryan quickly answered the call.

"I didn't see you last night," Donna said down the line.

"Yeah, sorry about that. I didn't finish until late and I didn't want to disturb you."

Ryan was aware of Donna having been so ill recently. She was still recovering from all the chemotherapy and surgery, and she needed her rest.

"I assume the late finish was down to that poor girl's body found near the bridge," she said.

"Yes, it was. It's now a murder investigation. She didn't jump."

"God, that's terrible," she said. "How old was she?"

"Seventeen."

"No age at all. Her family must be devastated."

Ryan always knew that whenever a loss like this happened—even when it was to someone else—it was impossible not to put themselves in the position of the victim's parents. Especially when it was a girl who'd been killed. He thought to who Hayley would have been at seventeen and if it was easier or harder to lose a child at an older age. Would it have been worse to have her in their lives for so long and then lose her, or would they have been grateful for those extra years? He didn't need to analyse that for too long. He definitely would have been grateful for those extra years.

"Do you think you'll be late again tonight?" she asked.

"Yes, most likely," he admitted, "but I would like to see you."

"I'd like to see you, too, but I understand if you have to work."

"I'll see what I can do and let you know later. How are you feeling?"

"A little tired," she said, "but I'm okay." She firmed her tone. "Really, Ryan. I am."

Though she'd been given the all clear, it was still hard not to worry. He imagined it must be a thousand times harder for Donna than it was for him. She was the one living in her body, who must still have cancer permanently on her mind. She must be constantly analysing every little twinge, paranoid for every potential lump, lying awake at night worrying about how it might next raise its ugly head.

"All right. I believe you. I'll give you a call later and let you know how I'm getting on."

"Speak later," she said and ended the call.

Ryan exhaled and stared at the phone for a moment.

Donna said she wanted to focus on the future now. Life had shown them too many times just how fragile it was, and she wanted to enjoy whatever time she had left on this earth. He wanted to embrace that point of view, but he struggled with it. Positivity wasn't something that came naturally to him. He hoped he wasn't being selfish by being back in her life. She deserved the absolute best of everything, and he wasn't able to put himself in that category.

"Everything all right, boss?" Mallory asked, bringing him out of it.

"Absolutely." He refocused his thoughts on the case. "Wish we'd got a bit more from the post-mortem."

"We know she wasn't sexually assaulted, so this wasn't a sexually motivated attack, and we know she took time to eat before she went to the bridge."

"Unless she ate before she left home?"

Mallory shook her head. "She didn't. I already asked her mother. She said Tai was going to eat with friends, she just didn't know who or where."

"Is it bad that I'm judging her for not knowing where her daughter was going or who she was with?"

"Tai was seventeen, almost eighteen. It's not like she was twelve."

He sighed and rubbed his hand across his face. "I know. I just have a feeling our jobs would be so much easier if we knew Tai's final movements."

RYAN HAD BARELY MADE it back to his desk before Linda hurried up to him.

"Boss, I've finished going through Tai's call log from the phone company. She had numerous calls and messages on the day she died, and the days leading up to her death, too."

"Anything interesting jumping out at you?"

"Actually, yes. She exchanged multiple phone calls from this number in the weeks up to when she died." She pushed a printed sheet with a list of dates, times, and numbers onto the desk in front of Ryan. "And one of the messages from the same number sounds strange."

She pointed to where it had been printed out.

What are we going to do?

"Not only that," Linda continued, "But Tai called the same number shortly after ten p.m. on the night she died."

"Do you know who the number belongs to?" Ryan asked.

"Yes, we've traced it back to one of the girls who goes to college with her, Chloe Jennings."

"It could just be a friend then. I imagine teenage girls talk to each other a lot. Have you tried to speak to her? Was she one of the people Shonda interviewed?"

Linda shook her head. "No, Shonda didn't interview her. I already asked. This is where it gets strange. She's not been into college since Monday, and no one has seen or heard from her. Doesn't look like she's posted on any of her social media accounts either."

"Okaaay," Ryan said slowly. "What about her family? Do they know where she is?"

"We can't get hold of anyone. Chloe's mother, Faye, doesn't appear to be anywhere to be found either. The mother's parents live in Cornwall, and I was able to get their home phone number, so I gave them a call to see if they were expecting Chloe and Faye for a visit, and they said they weren't. I didn't say too much else because I didn't want to worry them."

"They still could just be on holiday?"

"I thought the same, so I checked out both of their social media accounts—the obvious ones I could find—and neither of them have posted anything since the night Tai was killed. If they were going on holiday, don't you think they'd be posting photographs? Both of them were active, posting practically daily, up until a couple of nights ago."

That caught his interest. "What did you say their names were again?"

"Faye and Chloe Jennings."

"Any history we should be aware of?"

"No, nothing that comes up on the system. Faye Jennings has never had so much as a speeding ticket."

"Could just be a coincidence. They've taken a break from social media as well as from daily life."

Linda's blue eyes sparkled with excitement. It was clear she thought she was onto something important. "How many teenagers do you know who'd willingly take a break from social media? Plus, she hasn't mentioned having any kind of holiday coming up. She should be at college. She's missing lessons."

"What about Faye's work? What does she do for a living?"

"She works in social services. They didn't have any record of her having time off booked either."

Ryan pursed his lips. "So they've just upped and left around the same time another girl at the same college was killed. We can't pretend it's not suspicious."

"You agree with me that they might have something to do with Tai's death?"

"Honestly, I'm not sure at this point, but I do know that I don't believe in coincidences. Find out what car is registered to Faye Jennings and if it's missing as well, and then put a lookout on it. It might have been caught on a ANPR camera, and it'll give us an idea of where they've gone. There's the chance it's all perfectly innocent and they've just decided to take a break, but I'm not going to put any money on it."

"Can we do a welfare check on the house?" she asked.

"Yes, I think that's a good idea. We're not going to get a warrant on what we've got so far, but a welfare check should be fine." He thought for a moment, tapping his pen against his lips. "I wonder if Tai's mother, Lorraine, knew Chloe at all. Maybe she can give us an idea about what kind of relationship the girls had."

Linda nodded. "It's definitely worth asking the question."

"Agreed. I think I'll pay her a visit, get to meet her properly myself. Can you chase up digital forensics, see where they are with Tai's laptop. There might be something on there that will help, too."

Linda bobbed her head in a nod. "Will do."

Ryan glanced around the office, spotting his sergeant at the coffee machine.

Mallory had met Lorraine Moore and so had already developed a relationship. Ryan had only spoken to her in passing. It would be better if she came with him.

"You want to accompany me to interview Tai's mother again?" he asked her. "Something's come up."

Chapter Sixteen

"We're sorry to disturb you again," Ryan said as they settled into the worn sofa in Lorraine Moore's front room, "but something's come to light that we need to ask you about."

"About Tai?"

The woman looked about ten years older than the one in the many photographs around the room. They were all of her with Tai, at various ages, though, Ryan noticed, none were of Tai as a teenager. Her skin was sallow, her eyes hollowed. Her hand trembled as she lifted a cup of tea to her lips.

"It's connected to Tai, yes. Do you know a friend of hers called Chloe?"

Her brow creased in a frown. "Chloe Jennings?"

"Yes, that's right. You know her?"

"Chloe and Tai used to be friends in primary school. Best friends for a couple of years. Then they went to different secondary schools and grew apart."

"Did they stay in touch?"

"I think they did a bit, but only through social media or occasionally seeing each other at parties. Then they met up again when they started at the same college, but I'm not sure they were ever really friends again."

"How well did you know Tai's friends?"

A sad smile touched her lips, and a tear trickled from her eye. "When she was little, I knew her friends almost as well as I knew my own daughter. It felt like they were always around, having playdates or going to birthday parties. A lot of that was because us mums liked to get together, too, so we could have a moan about how hard parenting was, or how tired we were, or how much our other halves were pissing us off—not that I could really join in on that part. Then they left primary school, and the girls got more independent, and we all just stopped seeing each other. Got on with our lives, I guess. I met Richard, and you know how it is when you first meet someone. They consume all your time."

Ryan wondered how much time she'd had for her daughter. He didn't know what it was like to parent a teen, and he probably never would, but he imagined it must be a difficult balance between giving them the freedom to become their own, independent person, and not just allowing them to do whatever the hell they wanted.

"You said that you and the other mothers used to spend time together when the girls were younger. Does that mean you were close with Chloe's mum?"

She shrugged. "Faye? I suppose I was, at the time, but I'm sure she and all the others have heard about what's happened to Tai now, and not a single one has so much as sent me a text message to see how I'm holding up. It's not as though I'd have replied to them even if they had. I'd have known they were only contacting me because they wanted a bit of gossip to pass on. They're probably using my tragedy to make people feel sorry for them, saying how much Tai meant to them when they barely knew the young woman she'd become." Her voice broke, and she wiped away more tears, then she looked up and added, "I'm sorry. I don't understand what this has to do with Tai."

"Maybe nothing, but when we got Tai's phone records back, we noticed she and Chloe had been messaging each other regularly, and Tai called Chloe on the night she died."

"She did? I guess they were better friends than I thought. Does Chloe know something about what happened to Tai?"

"That's the thing." He took a breath. "We can't actually get hold of Chloe, and it appears her mother has gone, too."

"Gone? Where?"

"We don't know. When was the last time you spoke to Faye?"

She dragged her hand through her hair, thinking. "God, I really don't know. It's been years. We've commented on each other's Facebook posts occasionally, but that's about all. I don't understand. Do you think she knows something about what happened to Tai?"

"Honestly, we're not sure. It could be that she and Chloe have simply gone on holiday and the timing is strange."

She stared at him. "Do you believe that?"

"We have to look into all aspects of this case right now."

"Do they know who killed Tai? Have they gone on the run?"

Ryan held up both hands. "Slow down. We don't know what's happened yet. There could be a perfectly reasonable explanation for them leaving."

Her face flushed with colour. "If she had something to do with what happened to Tai, I'll kill her myself. I swear I will."

Mallory stepped in. "I understand you're upset, Lorraine, but there's no need for that."

She balled her fists and pressed them into her eyes, her shoulders shaking. "I just can't imagine what sick monster would want to end my baby's life. How am I supposed to live with this pain? I don't know if I can."

Ryan and Mallory exchanged a worried glance. It wasn't the first time Ryan had heard a devastated mother say that kind of thing, and he doubted it would be the last. He understood her pain. In a way, it was easier for parents who had other children they had to remain strong for—aware the murdered child's siblings were also heartbroken and trying to make sense of a world that had suddenly become a terrifying place.

As far as he could tell, the only person Lorraine had was Richard, and that wasn't accounting for much.

"I'll get in touch with the victim support team, make sure you have someone to talk to."

She shook her head. "What's the point? It won't bring Tai back."

"They can help you come to terms with what happened."

Her head snapped up. "Come to terms with it? How am I ever supposed to do that? My daughter was murdered! Have you got any idea what I'm going through?"

Ryan cleared his throat and stared down at where his fingers were linked between his knees. "My daughter was killed by a drunk driver a few years ago. He mowed her down right in front of me and drove off. So, yes, I do know what you're going through."

She clapped her hand to her mouth. "God, I'm so sorry, Detective. I shouldn't have said that."

"It's perfectly okay. Like I said, I understand. It does get easier. The pain, it's always there, but it's less raw. You learn how to function again."

"Before she went out that evening, I wish I'd said a proper goodbye. I wish I'd hugged her and told her I loved her, or even that I'd told her she couldn't go anywhere. I should have. It was a school night. I should have told her she needed to stay home." She gave a choked laugh. "Not that she would have listened to me. She would have told me that I couldn't make her do anything, and she was right, I couldn't. Tai did whatever she wanted, and I was this pathetic bleating voice in the background that she basically just ignored."

"I'm sure that's not true," Mallory said.

"I blame myself." Lorraine wiped at her eyes, but tears continued to stream down her cheeks. "I knew something was wrong. I've known for weeks. I kept telling myself that it was all part of her being a moody teen."

Mallory handed her a packet of tissues from her bag, and she accepted them gratefully.

"What made you think something was wrong?" Mallory asked.

"She was even moodier than normal, and secretive, too. I'd hear her talking on her phone to someone, and when I'd knock, she'd go quiet and yell out 'what?' at me. Her temper was so explosive, I was frightened to say or do the wrong thing."

"Teenagers can be like that. You weren't to know."

"If only I'd talked to her more. If only I'd been a different kind of parent. I've been distracted by Richard. I'll be honest, I've been selfish. I thought about my own life and happiness and put it before hers. I shouldn't have done that. I thought she'd be moving out of home any day now and then I'd be stuck here all alone." Her tears grew harsher. "Now I'm going to grow old without my daughter. What's the point in that? I've got no reason to be here anymore."

"Please, don't say things like that," Mallory urged. "Time will make things easier. I know that's hard to believe right now, but you'll learn to live with it."

They sat in silence for a moment, allowing Lorraine to gather herself again.

Ryan cleared his throat. Lorraine probably wasn't going to want to talk about this, but, after meeting her boyfriend earlier that day, he needed to put some feelers around it.

"Richard mentioned that he and Tai argued at times," he said. "You didn't notice anything secretive happening between the two of them?"

Her eyes widened, the tears drying up almost instantly. "What are you saying?"

Ryan put his elbows on his knees and leaned forwards slightly. "Tai was living with a man she wasn't related to, who was possibly closer to her age than yours. You have to understand that we need to explore the possibility there was more to the relationship."

"No! Absolutely not. I can't believe you'd say that. He's older than her! A lot older. Just because he's younger than me doesn't mean that he'd be sleeping with my daughter. Jesus Christ." She put her head in her hands, her fingers clawing into her dishevelled hair.

"I'm sorry, I didn't mean to upset you. These are questions we really have to ask. We know Richard spent time in prison for drug dealing. Were you aware of his past when you got involved with him?"

"Not initially, no, but he told me eventually."

"When did he tell you?"

She shifted uncomfortably in her seat. "A friend of mine was getting married in the States and wanted us to come. Richard said he couldn't go and made up lots of excuses, most of which I was able to navigate. Then he admitted that he couldn't go to America because they wouldn't let him in the country because he'd served time for drugs."

"When was this?"

"About six months after we first met. He was already living here by then."

Ryan nodded. "Richard moved in fairly quickly, didn't he?"

"We knew we loved each other, and as you've pointed out, I'm not getting any younger. It seemed silly him keeping his flat and us paying twice when he was here most of the time anyway."

"Is there any chance Richard is still involved with drugs? Could he have got Tai involved as well?"

She sat back and threw up her hands. "What's wrong with you people? We're a normal family. We're not some den of iniquity."

"Of course not, but we have to ask. We're not doing our jobs if we don't, and I'm sure you want to find out what's behind your daughter's death as much as we do."

Maybe she didn't, Ryan wondered. Perhaps Lorraine Moore was one of those people who would rather stick their heads in the sand than learn the truth. She'd said herself that she'd known something was wrong with Tai but hadn't wanted to ask. Could it be the same for Richard?

"I don't know what more you want from me. I've told you everything I know. I've even given you Tai's laptop in the hope it would help. I'm not hiding anything from you, and neither is Richard."

"We really appreciate your cooperation," Ryan said, trying to smooth things over. "And thanks for letting us have Tai's laptop. We have our digital forensics team working on it now, but we'll get it back to you as soon as we can."

She sniffed. "I don't know what you think you'll find on there."

"If we can access her social media and messages, we might get a good idea about who she was meeting the night she died."

Not only that, they might be able to work out what it was that had Tai's mother thinking there was something wrong in the weeks leading up to her murder.

"Would it be okay if we took a look at Tai's room?" he asked.

"Your colleagues did that the day she was found."

"I know. I just want to get a feel for it myself. Try to understand a little more what kind of person Tai was."

Lorraine sniffed and nodded. "Sure. Come with me."

She rose from her chair like an old woman, pushing herself up using the armrest and then shuffling across the carpet. She was only in her forties, but grief had her moving like she was eighty.

Ryan followed her up the stairs and across the landing to one of the bedrooms. The door was shut, but Lorraine opened it, and then moved back to allow the detectives through.

"Do we have your permission to look through Tai's belongings?" he asked.

"I guess so. What harm can it do now?"

They stepped into the bedroom, and automatically took their gloves from their pockets to cover their hands. The room was messy, with clothes and makeup everywhere and the bed unmade. Ryan assumed the room hadn't been touched since Tai's death.

Mallory went to the wardrobe and opened the door, flicking through the clothes hanging there, checking at the back of it for anything that might have been hidden.

"Tai has a lot of nice things," Mallory said to Lorraine.

"Oh, yes. Her appearance was important to her."

"She didn't have a job or anything, you know, to pay for it all?"

Lorraine shook her head. "No, I wanted her to focus on her studies. We spend the rest of our lives working, don't we?"

"Did she get an allowance then?"

"Yes, fifty quid a month, but she had to help me around the house, run the hoover around, do her washing and put it away, that kind of thing."

Ryan wondered where Mallory was going with this. To him, it just looked like any other teenage girl's room.

"I think we've seen enough," Mallory said. "Thank you for your time."

It was clear Mallory wanted to say something to him without Lorraine overhearing, so he went with it.

"If you do happen to hear from Faye Jennings, or even Chloe Jennings," he said to Lorraine, "will you let us know?"

"Of course."

Ryan and Mallory left the house and headed back to the car.

"Did you see the room?" Mallory asked.

Ryan frowned. She knew he'd seen the room—she'd been right there with him.

"What do you mean?"

"I had a quick look through her wardrobe. That girl had money. *Bougie*, I believe the lifestyle is called these days. Expensive makeup, branded clothing, I even spotted a couple of expensive pieces of jewellery."

"Maybe they're presents. Lorraine might have bought them for her."

"Lorraine doesn't seem like the sort of person who has that kind of money to flash around. They live in a two-bedroom flat in Brislington. She works as a school receptionist. Hardly rolling in it."

"They had enough to consider a trip to America," he pointed out.

"True. But maybe they'd been saving. If they were saving, they definitely wouldn't be spending on branded clothes and foundations that cost a hundred quid a bottle."

Ryan's jaw dropped. "A hundred quid a bottle? People don't really pay that sort of money for something that gets wiped off at the end of the day?"

"They do, but they're not normally teenagers."

He frowned. "What are you thinking?"

"That maybe Tai had a boyfriend we don't know about—someone who's been buying her gifts. Her mother said that she'd been secretive recently, talking to someone on the phone and going silent when she thought her mother was near."

Ryan tapped his finger against his lips. "Possibly, or she was into shoplifting. Or perhaps she was making money another way. We already know Tai has connection with someone with past drug convictions."

"You're thinking county lines?"

"Possibly. She might have been running drugs and getting the extra money that way."

"We need the information from her laptop from digital forensics as soon as possible. Hopefully, we'll be able to get some clues from that."

He blew out a breath. "If only we'd been able to locate her phone."

"If it's county lines," Mallory said, "aren't they normally given burner phones?"

"You think she might have a second mobile somewhere?"

"It's a possibility. There might be money hidden somewhere, too."

"We'll have to ask her mother if we can search her room properly, or else we'll need a warrant."

"Lorraine is going to want to know why, and no grieving mother wants to hear that her daughter was caught up in something like drug running."

He bit his lower lip. "We don't need to tell her our suspicions, and that's really all they are right now. But someone killed Tai, and there's a good chance it wasn't a random act. What was she doing up on the bridge that night? From our questioning so far, it doesn't look as though she was meeting a friend. That end of the bridge is basically the start of Somerset county. Might she have been there to meet someone she was running drugs for?"

Mallory fell silent as she thought for a moment. "Why would they ask to meet somewhere they must know there are cameras? Why not just meet a little farther down, where there aren't any? The only reason someone would have to meet her there is because they'd already planned to kill her."

She was right.

"Maybe she upset the wrong people—decided to out them or something."

Mallory continued. "And what's the connection between the Jenningses going missing and Tai being killed? Could they be involved as well?"

Ryan ran his hand through his hair and shook his head. "Honestly, I have no idea at this stage, and I don't like it when I have no idea. I don't believe Faye and Chloe Jennings going missing around the same time as Tai is killed can be a coincidence. My gut tells me Faye and her daughter have run for a reason. It's up to us to figure out what that reason is. They could be in danger as well, or perhaps they're the ones running from the police. Either way, we need to find them."

Chapter Seventeen

Faye had been driving all day, and she still didn't have an exact location she was heading towards apart from generally aiming north to put as many miles between them and Bristol as possible. She was also aware that she needed to change the car. The number plate was going to get them spotted. It would leave a trail for the police to follow.

She wasn't sure how she was going to sort the car situation out. She had some cash, but they needed that to live on, and whoever she bought a car from would need to be the kind of person who wouldn't ask too many questions.

If only she'd had an up-to-date passport for Chloe, then they'd have been able to get out of the country. She'd never previously thought of the UK as being particularly small, but suddenly it felt tiny. When you could drive the entire length of it in less than a day, it didn't feel like the sort of place to get lost in. They'd have been much better off in Europe, vanishing into the Bulgarian countryside or somewhere like that, but there was no point in getting wistful over the impossible.

Maybe if she found someone dodgy enough to sell her a car without seeing any identification they would also be the kind of person who would know where to get fake passports from.

She rolled her eyes at herself. That kind of thing was what you saw in films, it didn't actually happen for people like them.

Chloe had spent most of the day dozing in the passenger seat or complaining she was bored. Without her phone, she no longer had use of the AirPods that were normally superglued to her ears, and apparently, the radio—even Radio One—only played crap music. Plus, the DJs talked too much. Faye wasn't going to argue with her daughter about that one.

The whole time she'd been driving, she found herself glancing into the rearview mirror, constantly watching out for any signs of a car following her or that the person who'd caught her attention at the bed and breakfast was behind the wheel.

"Can we stop soon?" Chloe moaned. "I'm so bored, I might actually die."

They had been on the road a long time. It felt safer to keep moving, but they did have to find somewhere to stop for the night.

"Okay, fine. We'll start looking for somewhere to stay."

Chloe slumped back in her seat. "Ugh. Thank God."

That bristle of irritation went through Faye again. There was a reason they were in this situation, and Chloe didn't seem to appreciate it. It wasn't as though they were on a road trip for the fun of it.

Was there something wrong with her daughter? She'd never thought such a thing before, but now she couldn't help but question if Chloe was emotionally stunted or something? How could she not be a wreck right now? Faye felt like she'd been hollowed out. Constant tears hovered beneath the surface, ready to burst out if anyone showed her even a moment of kindness. She didn't seem able to get hold of her trembling, and feelings of anxiety and fear overwhelmed her.

By contrast, Chloe didn't seem any different to normal.

Was this Chloe's way of coping with the fear and shock? Just by shutting down to protect herself from the emotion? Faye wanted to believe that was the reason for her daughter's apathy. It wasn't as though this behaviour was normal—but then neither was the situation.

She checked the rearview mirror again.

Her heart stuttered.

A man was in the car directly behind them. Was it the same one she'd seen at the bed and breakfast? It was hard to tell, but something about him made her heart race.

A car in front stopped suddenly.

She slammed on the brakes, throwing out her left arm to protect her daughter from the crash she felt sure was imminent.

"Mum!" Chloe cried.

Faye blew out a breath. "Shit."

Her shaking intensified. They were lucky the man in the car hadn't gone straight into the back of them.

The man in the car!

She twisted in her seat. He caught her eye and threw up both his hands and mouthed 'what the hell' at her. She understood why—she'd stopped out of nowhere. She also now saw that the man driving looked nothing like the one who'd been at the B&B.

"What were you doing? You definitely weren't watching the road." Chloe turned around. "You were looking at the car behind us, weren't you? Or at least not the car, but the man driving it."

Her daughter had seen right through her, and Faye swallowed nervously.

"Maybe."

Even if it wasn't him, it might be someone he'd sent. It wasn't as though he'd be working alone. That was the frightening part. She didn't know who she could trust. Every face she saw as she walked the street could potentially belong to one of them.

"Mum, stop it!"

She glanced over to where Chloe was staring at her, her eyes wide, eyebrows lifted high, in that way people did when they were trying to convey something they couldn't say out loud.

"What?"

"Not every man is going to be a threat."

She was right, there were women who got involved as well.

"My job is to protect you, and I've done a spectacularly bad job of that so far." Unbidden tears filled her eyes, and she blinked them back. "So excuse me if I overreact a little every now and then."

"You didn't do a bad job of it. I'm my own person. I created my own problems. It isn't your fault."

"I was lazy. I knew something wasn't right, but I just brushed it off. I didn't want to believe there might be something wrong or something to worry about."

Chloe shook her head. "It isn't your fault, Mum."

"I'm your mother. I'm supposed to protect you."

Behind them, the man honked his horn. She was holding up the traffic now, but she was still shaky, her legs feeling like they didn't really belong to her. Was she even safe to drive?

But she couldn't just sit here, blocking up the road, so she forced herself to put the car into gear and put her foot on the accelerator. The car she'd almost hit was long gone, but the one that had distracted her was still behind her.

She drove with her fingers gripped around the steering wheel, her knuckles white. The muscles in her shoulders were bunched into knots, and she could tell she was hunched over but couldn't bring herself to sit back.

"I'm going to have to pull over for a minute. Take a breather."

"Sure, Mum. Whatever you need."

What she needed was to be able to go back in time and change what had happened, but such a thing was impossible.

Chapter Eighteen

B ack in the office, Ryan called all his team members to the incident room.

He'd found photographs of the mother and daughter from social media and printed them out for the incident board. A line connected them to the photograph of Tai.

"Faye Jennings is forty-six years old and works in social services. She has no priors. Her daughter is seventeen-year-old Chloe Jennings. The family used to be close with the Moores when the girls were at primary school but lost touch after the girls went to different secondary schools. This year, Tai and Chloe both started at Bristol College. They're studying different courses—Tai was doing a vocational course in marketing while Chloe is taking A levels—but they met up again at some point. We know this because on Tai's phone records there are a number of calls between the two girls on the following dates over the past three months, including one that lasted for twelve minutes shortly after ten p.m. on the night Tai died." He paused long enough to hand out printouts of the call dates to his team. "Plus, there are messages, including one from earlier that same day."

He'd blown the screenshot of the message up and printed it out to pin next to Chloe's photograph.

What are we going to do?

He tapped the printout with his finger. "I don't know about you, but to me that sounds like a message from a girl in trouble."

Members of his team nodded in agreement.

"We have to ask ourselves what kind of trouble? And was it enough for someone to kill Tai over?" He took a couple of paces. "On Tuesday morning, sometime after Tai was thrown from the Clifton Suspension Bridge, Chloe and her mother, Faye, went dark and no one has seen or heard from them since. Faye didn't have any leave booked and hasn't been in touch with her employers, and Chloe hasn't told the college that she's going away either. I'm sure I don't need to tell any of you how suspicious that appears. Faye drives a silver twenty-nineteen Nissan Qashqai with the following number plate." It was also printed and pinned to the wall. "A welfare check to the house has shown the car is missing from the family's driveway and doesn't appear to be parked on any of the adjoining roads, so let's assume it's what they left in. Whether they're still driving it or not, we don't know. Either way, I want a lookout put on the vehicle. They could be anywhere in the country or might have even left it by now."

He focused on one of his team members. "Linda, can you check if they've got valid passports, and if so, see if they've been used recently."

"Yes, boss."

Craig lifted a hand and spoke up. "Is it possible they've gone on holiday? Maybe they heard about Tai's death and wanted to get away without telling anyone?"

"It's always a possibility, but for a woman who's never taken a sick day to just not show up at work, I'd say it's unlikely."

Dev Kharral tapped his foot as he spoke. "Is it worth trying to get a warrant to search their house? What about getting their phone records?"

"During the welfare check, we noticed two mobile phones and laptops in the house, but obviously, without a warrant, we were unable to do anything with them. I will attempt to get said warrant, but right now, I don't think we've got enough to get one. We don't actually know what we'd be searching for—but we might be able to request the phone records of both Chloe and Faye. Right now, all we have is a text message linking Chloe to Tai, and the phone calls, but two college girls calling each other is hardly unusual." He thought for a moment. "Let's interview the neighbours, see if they noticed Chloe and Faye leaving the house early Tuesday morning. Might be worth finding out if they ever saw Tai coming and going from Chloe's house, too."

He paused to let his team take notes.

"I think we need to talk to both of their friends—the mother's and the daughter's. Shonda, since you've already been making inroads in the friendship group, can I get you to deal with that."

Shonda nodded.

"Find out who Chloe hangs out with at college," Ryan said. "She may have spoken to someone other than Tai if something's been bothering her. Ask about the connection between Tai and Chloe—did they see much of each other at college? What kind of student is Chloe? Any problems with drink or drugs? Do their peers consider them to be friends? Speak to Faye's friends and colleagues as well. Has she been worried about Chloe?"

"I spoke to one of Tai's classmates, and word is that Tai has an older man in her life," Shonda said. "A boyfriend who buys her whatever she wants."

Mallory turned to Shonda. "We found expensive clothes, makeup, and jewellery in Tai's room, which lines up with what her friends have said."

"Could it be Richard who bought her those things?" Shonda suggested.

Ryan pursed his lips. "Possibly, though we can't forget that he has an alibi for the night she was killed. An alibi in the form of Tai's mother. Maybe she's protecting him, but I struggle to believe that. I can't see a mother protecting her daughter's killer."

Mallory turned back to Ryan. "He might have told her that he was doing something else that he doesn't want us to know about. Maybe she believed him and covered for him anyway."

"Plus, he has a record for drug dealing," Craig pointed out. "If Tai was involved in that as well, he might have been the person who got her into it. Someone higher up the pecking order could have been the one to actually kill her."

Ryan rubbed his fingers across his mouth. "The problem is that all this is theory—except Richard's record, of course. We don't have any proof of anything yet. We've got a bit of blurry CCTV footage, but that's all. If it wasn't Richard who bought her those things, who did, and what's the connection with Chloe? Did Tai have her own bank account? I'm assuming she did at her age? Can we request her account details, see what her spending was like?"

"If someone else bought her these things," Shonda said, "it's not going to show up on her bank account."

"True," Ryan said, "but it's worth trying. Something might come up that seems suspicious."

He checked his watch. It was already getting late. "We're not going to have time to make much more progress on this tonight, but I want everyone to get a good night's sleep and jump straight in first thing in the morning."

Chapter Nineteen

Mallory left the office and headed to her car. Her head was down as she rifled in her bag for her keys, so it wasn't until she almost reached the vehicle that she stopped short.

Someone was waiting beside her car.

She realised who the person was, and her heart sank. Shit. Daniel. What the hell was he doing here? She remembered how he hadn't turned up for his shift with Oliver. The truth was, she'd barely given it a second thought all day, too preoccupied with the case for it to be at the forefront of her mind.

She hesitated, tempted to turn on her heel and go straight back into work. But he'd already seen her, and if she did that, she'd look like she was running away. She didn't want him to think she was frightened of him or that he'd won in any way. It was also kind of embarrassing that someone she'd got involved with would go to the extent of tracking her down to her place of work. She was aware that because she lived with Oliver and had to take his needs into consideration, that sometimes impinged upon her job, and she always did her best to try to keep her home and work life as separate as possible. She'd hate to think of people whispering around the office that she wasn't pulling her weight because she was distracted by personal issues. Having one of those such issues show up in the car park was the last thing she wanted.

Setting her shoulders and lifting her chin, she marched over to her car, coming to a stop on the opposite side of it to Daniel, so the car bonnet was between them.

"Daniel, you know this is a police station," she started before he could get a word in. "My colleagues are all in the building behind us, and I don't think they'd be impressed if I told them you were hassling me right now."

He regarded her coolly. "Hello, Mallory. Nice to see you, too."

"It's *not* nice to see you. Not at all. What are you doing here?"

"What do you think I'm doing here? You contacted my work and had me replaced? I'm off for one shift and you report me to my boss?"

Her stomach knotted. In her job, she wasn't afraid of confrontation, but it was different when it was to do with work rather than it being personal. She told herself this shouldn't be personal. She needed to keep things professional. It wasn't easy, though.

She steadied herself with a breath. "Daniel, there are clearly issues between us. It wasn't just about the missed shift and you know it. I wasn't comfortable with you showing up at my house the other night, unannounced, and now you're here as well. I don't need to remind you that I'm a police officer, and I'm not going to put up with inappropriate behaviour."

"Is that a threat?" he said. "I *had* to turn up at your house because you wouldn't talk to me. You didn't leave me with any other choice."

"I don't owe you my time, Daniel."

He flapped a hand. "You don't owe me your time? Are you serious? How fucking full of yourself can you get? I spent months with Oliver when you were too busy with your job, and this is how you repay me?"

"It was *your* job to spend time with Oliver. You didn't do it out of the goodness of your heart."

"I always stayed longer than I was scheduled to. I did that for you, Mallory, because I knew you always worked late and you'd feel better knowing someone was with Oliver."

She experienced a twinge of guilt. Was she overreacting? Had she been too hard on him?

He continued, "It's obvious to me that you're always going to put your *career* before anyone else."

The way he said 'career' instantly expunged any feeling of guilt. He'd put a sneer on it, as though it was something bad, something that should be mocked. Mallory was proud of what she did. She'd never done particularly well at school, or been popular, but she'd made something of herself. The way she spent her days was important, and it made a difference to people's lives. She'd sacrificed her personal life, both for her job and for her brother.

"I'm not going to apologise to you for the way I've lived my life. I appreciate the time you spent with Ollie, and I know he's going to miss you, but things haven't worked out. You need to accept that and move on."

He glared at her. "Fine. You're really not that important to me anyway, Mallory. I only took you out for those drinks because I thought you might have been easy. You look the type.

Beneath the suit, I've seen the tattoos and piercings. Women like you normally put out."

She clenched her fists. "Right, that's enough. This conversation ends now. I don't want to hear from you again, and that's final."

Inside, she boiled with humiliation and anger. How dare he think it was okay for him to speak to her like that. Was that really how people saw her? She might have a slightly alternative style, but she'd always thought people respected her. The thought that they might somehow see her as less of a police officer simply because she had a few extra pierced holes and had some tattoos hidden beneath her shirtsleeves and her hair was dyed, the fringe cut a little too short, unnerved her.

But Daniel still wasn't done. "You don't want to hear from me? Who says you get to have that choice?"

She gestured to the building behind her. "The police, that's who. It's called harassment, and it's against the law."

He shook his head at her, as though she was something that disgusted him. "Does it make you feel like a big person, Mallory? Like you're someone important? So you're going to set your police officer friends on me now, are you?"

The truth was, the last people she wanted to get involved with this were her work colleagues. The thought of them seeing this confrontation left her mortified. She just wanted to shrink into nothing and vanish.

"I will if you don't leave."

"Fuck you, Mallory," Daniel said before turning and stomping off to his car.

She stayed where she was until he'd climbed in and driven off, and then her whole body sagged. She lifted her car keys to hit the button on the fob to unlock it and realised her hand was shaking.

Someone came up behind her, and she jumped, her hand clutched to her chest. "Oh God."

It was Ryan.

He frowned at her. "You all right?"

She forced a smile. "Of course."

She wasn't going to let Daniel get to her. She was kicking herself now for ever giving him the wrong idea about things. She refused to let his opinions change how she thought about herself.

"You sure? I thought I saw you talking to someone."

"Oh, just the carer who was helping out with Ollie. He's not working there now. He just came to say goodbye. I won't be seeing him again."

"Things didn't work out?" he enquired.

"No, but it's fine."

She wasn't sure why she hadn't told the truth. Was she ashamed of how Daniel had treated her? Or was it that she was ashamed of how she had treated Daniel?

"Have you got a replacement lined up?" Ryan asked. "Is Oliver managing okay?"

"Not yet, but we'll be fine. He's been so much better recently. I can't even remember the last time he had a nightmare and he's back in the kitchen, cooking for himself. It's like the fire never happened."

Ryan offered her a smile. "That's great news. I was a bit worried for you both for a while there."

"Well, I was worried about you, too, so I guess that makes two of us."

"Hopefully, things are on the up for us both then. Goodnight, Mallory."

She nodded and opened her car door. "See you tomorrow."

Chapter Twenty

Ryan was grateful he didn't have to go back to his crappy flat this evening. He'd slipped a couple of work shirts into the wardrobe in Donna's spare room and hoped she wouldn't notice. He didn't want her to think he was trying to move back in surreptitiously.

It was strange being back in the house, though. Everywhere he looked were reminders of the life he'd once shared with both Donna and Hayley. A framed painting on the wall, bought directly from the artist at a market in Edinburgh when they'd done a trip to Scotland. There was the giant set of shelves in the dining room that he and Donna had fought over—she'd found them at a reclaimed furniture place and had fallen in love, but he'd insisted they were far too big for the room. Donna had obviously won that fight.

But there were also reminders everywhere of the years he hadn't been in the house. He hated to think that Donna's ex, Tony, had left his mark here as well. It was especially hard not to think of him in her bed. He wished he was into some kind of woo-woo and could bring a sage bundle or something into the house to smoke out any remaining Tony vibes. But that wasn't really Ryan's style.

Ryan had to keep catching himself from thinking 'when I move back in'. He didn't want to take it for granted that moving back into the house was on the cards. He loved Donna—he always had—but she'd been through a lot. The last thing she needed was him putting extra pressure on her. She probably needed to figure out who she was after the cancer had put such a massive strain on her body, the physical changes that he knew had affected her mentally as well.

He rang the bell—something he still found weird as he couldn't shake the feeling that this house was still his, even though Donna had bought him out of his share years ago—and waited.

A few seconds passed before she opened the door, smiling at him. She was pleased to see him, and that meant a lot. There was a while after they'd first separated when she hadn't even been able to stand being in his company. Actually, neither of them had been able to bear it. The weight of each other's grief had been too much, and with Ryan's grief was also guilt. Could he have done something differently to prevent their daughter's death? He knew if he was thinking it, then those thoughts must have crossed Donna's mind as well.

It occurred to him that maybe he should have been more sympathetic with Richard going to work instead of staying home to take care of Lorraine? While Ryan hadn't gone back to work the day after Hayley's death, it hadn't been too long after. He'd wanted to escape as well.

"Hi." He leaned down and kissed her mouth.

"Hi, yourself. How was work?" she asked, letting him in.

"Busy as always. You don't want to hear about it, I'm sure."

One of the things she'd often complained about during their marriage was how he always dominated their conversations with work. It was a struggle not to, though. It took up such a massive part of his life that it left him floundering for conversation, trying to figure out what else he could say.

"How's your day been?" he said instead.

"Quiet." She led him through into the kitchen. "Wine?"

"Just a small one. I'm driving."

"You might not need to drive anywhere."

Was there flirtation in her words? It was what he wanted to hear.

He grinned. "No? Make it a decent-sized one then." He sniffed the air. "Something smells good."

"Homemade beef stroganoff. I've had it in the slow cooker all day, so the beef should be really tender."

"Sounds amazing."

She went to the cupboard and selected a bottle of red. "Since we're having beef," she explained.

She took out two glasses and poured them both a generous amount. He took that as an indication she was happy for him to stay the night, as he obviously wouldn't be driving.

"Are you hungry yet? It's ready, if you are."

"Starving. I had a crappy supermarket sandwich about eight hours ago, and I've basically been living on coffee and biscuits since then."

She motioned to the kitchen table. "Sit then. I've done rice with it. Hope that's okay."

"You didn't need to do all of this. We could have ordered a takeaway."

He felt guilty that she'd cooked for him when she should have been resting.

"I like to do it. Gives me a distraction."

He took a sip of his wine as she dished up. The air was filled with the savoury aroma of beef, onions, and garlic.

She set a plate down in front of him and one for herself.

"This looks great," he said.

There was something to be said for coming home to a smiling face and a homecooked meal. He'd take it over his cold, empty flat and his shitty meals for one any day.

Donna smiled. "Don't let it get cold."

Ryan got stuck in, suddenly realising just how hungry he was. Donna had been right, the beef was tender, and the rice was light and fluffy. He probably ate too fast but cleared his plate and sat back with his hands over his still-flat stomach.

He stayed quiet until Donna had finished and set her knife and fork down.

He picked up his wine and took another sip. "I'm a bit concerned about Mallory."

She put her elbows on the table and cupped her chin in her palm. "Oh? In what way?"

"She doesn't seem herself."

"She's got a lot on her plate, what with working as a detective sergeant and taking care of her brother. They had that fire not too long ago as well, didn't they?"

"Yes, but she said things are much better now. Ollie was pretty traumatised at the time and wasn't sleeping and was suffering from night terrors, but Mallory coped, just about. Now she seems...distant. Worried. Though she keeps insisting everything is fine."

"Man trouble then?" she suggested.

He frowned. "Could be. She was seeing someone who helped Oliver out during the times when she wasn't home for longer shifts. I thought it was all over between them—I think it was only ever a couple of drinks, you know, nothing serious, but I did see him talking to her next to her car earlier."

"You don't think he's giving her any grief, do you?"

"Mallory is pretty good at handling herself. She's very capable."

Donna shrugged. "Even capable women need watching out for at times."

"You're right. I'll talk to her again in the morning, see if I can figure out what's going on with her. I just don't want her to think I'm prying into something that's none of my business."

"It doesn't do any harm to ask, let her know that you're there for her, if she needs you, and that she can always come and talk to you without fear of judgement."

"Thanks, Donna. I will."

He hoped Mallory was already aware that he'd be there for her, but he also knew he had a habit of assuming people realised how he felt without actually saying it out loud. He was probably doing the same thing right now with Donna, but he was too frightened of rejection to tell her that he wanted to move back in sooner rather than later.

He changed the subject. "Have you got any plans to go back to work now you're feeling better?"

"I'm doing a bit from home." She swirled her hand beside her head. "It's good to keep my brain occupied. Too much time to think isn't healthy."

"Resting is, though."

"I'm not sick anymore, Ryan."

"No, but you're still recovering."

She sighed. "It's hard not to overanalyse everything, you know? The slightest little pain or feeling more tired than normal. I feel like I'm on stolen time and the cancer is just going to come back to reclaim it from me."

"You don't know that. The doctors said there was only an eight percent chance of it returning. You have this time now. You can't waste it by worrying."

She gave a sad smile. "It's easy for you to say. You can escape it. I'm trapped in this body. It's with me constantly."

Her words broke his heart. He wanted to say or do something to make it better—he was a fixer by nature—but there was nothing he could say. Anything he thought of felt like putting a plaster over a cracked skull.

He reached across the table and took her hand. Then stood and went around to her side and tugged her to standing. He kissed her and then pulled her in for a hug, placing his nose against the softness of her regrowing hair.

"How about you go and sit in the lounge and finish your wine, while I do the dishes?" he said.

She smiled. "And then we can go to bed? I could do with you taking my mind off things."

He kissed her again. "That, I can definitely do."

Chapter Twenty-One

Faye squinted against the early morning sunshine and checked to make sure she had the right place.

The small car sales garage was set off a narrow country lane. The forecourt contained around ten vehicles, and another few were positioned behind the dirty glass windows of the showroom. The structure itself appeared to be wooden with the white paint peeling. A portacabin served as an office.

Faye had never felt so self-conscious. What the hell was she thinking, doing this? How had her life gone in this direction? She wished she could just forget the whole thing and turn around and go home but she couldn't. It was too dangerous. She needed to be brave, and if that meant having some secondhand salesman treat her like shit, then that's just what she had to put up with. She'd left Chloe back at the B&B, but even doing that made her anxious. Everywhere she looked held the potential of a threat. She'd instructed Chloe not to answer the door to anyone, but, as recent times had proven, Chloe couldn't always be trusted.

Moving slowly, she wandered around the cars, peering inside windows, though she wasn't totally sure what she wanted.

The door of the portacabin opened. She must have been spotted.

The man was around her age—short and skinny and prematurely balding. He wore a cheap suit that really wasn't necessary considering the state of his forecourt. There wasn't a single vehicle worth more than a couple of grand.

"Can I help you?" The Scottish burr was thick and warm and didn't seem to fit the person it belonged to.

"Umm...I'm not sure. Maybe."

She was hugely aware of her accent and how it made her stand out as not being local. She was sure it wasn't true that the Scottish didn't like the English—at least she *hoped* it wasn't true.

She thought constantly of the trail she was leaving. The cash she'd withdrawn from her two bank accounts before they'd left already seemed to be running low. Nothing was cheap anymore, and each time she had to fill the car with fuel, or buy them something to eat, or pay for a room for the night, the less money they had. She hadn't been able to empty her accounts because that kind of thing got flagged up as fraud these days. The bank manager would have asked her too many questions—perhaps thinking she'd fallen victim to one of those Arabian prince emails—and she hadn't had the time or the inclination to answer them. It had been easier just to withdraw what she could from the cashpoint and hope things sorted themselves out before the money ran out. She was fully aware that if she was forced to use her credit card at any point, it would leave a trail for someone to follow.

"Got your eye on anything nice?" he asked

She didn't give a shit what kind of car she ended up driving, just as long as it wasn't going to break down on her anytime soon.

How long did it take to register a car? It would take a few days for the police to follow the paper trail, she was sure. All she knew was that she needed to get rid of her old car and buy herself some time.

"I wondered if you'd be interested in doing a part exchange for my car?" She nodded over to her 2019 Nissan Qashqai.

He sucked air in over his teeth. "Sorry, but I'm not exactly cash rich right now. I wouldn't be able to afford something like that."

"I'm happy to take a low price," she said, feeling desperate.

"It's not been a good season. I'm doing sales only, sorry."

She didn't have the money to pay for a vehicle either, but she needed to get rid of her Qashqai.

"What about a straight trade?"

He narrowed his eyes. "You want to trade in that for one of my vehicles?"

"That's right."

"It's not stolen, is it?"

She almost laughed. "Do I look like someone who would steal a car? No, I promise. It's all legit. I just need...something different."

He seemed suspicious, understandably so. But she still needed to try.

"I can sign it over to you, but I just ask that you wait a few days before you try to register yourself as the new owner."

"Why?"

"I-I'm trying to leave my husband. He's been abusing me, and I've just built up the courage to finally take our daughter and run."

His eyes widened. "Your husband has been hitting you?"

She discovered it wasn't difficult to conjure some tears. The stress of the past few days, combined with her not having a full night's sleep since everything had happened, had left her emotional and tearful. She pictured how she must appear to this man—some exhausted, middle-aged woman, begging him to swap a car worth substantially more than one of his with him.

Would he call the police once she'd left?

A shot of fear went through her. She couldn't have that happen. All at once, she regretted coming here. What had she been thinking? She should have just dumped her car and they could have travelled using public transport. That would have been safer.

She took a step back. "It's okay. I've changed my mind. Forget I said anything."

He put a hand out to her. "Hang on, wait a sec."

She shrank back, and he snatched the hand down again. "Please, I didn't mean to upset you. If you think it'll help you, I can do that."

It probably didn't hurt that he was making a good couple of grand on the deal. He'd be able to sell her car on for a hell of a lot more than he would one of the bangers currently sitting on his forecourt. He couldn't pretend he was being completely altruistic.

"As long as I'm not going to get your husband accusing me of trying to sell his car," he added.

"The car is all in my name. I promise. I wouldn't put you in that position."

She was telling the truth.

"And you'll wait a few days before trying to transfer any paperwork? You promise? If he figures out where I've been, he'll come after me, and there's a good chance he might kill me."

"Don't you think you should call the police?"

"I'll be dead before the police can do anything."

She was telling the truth about that part, too.

"Can I take a closer look at it?" he asked.

"Of course."

She stepped a little closer and handed him the keys. That was a stupid move. What was stopping him from just stealing her car now? She'd already said she didn't want to get the police involved, so she wasn't likely to call them about a stolen car either.

He nodded and clutched the keys and approached her Nissan. Her stomach clenched again, and she had to stop herself doubling over. Though she knew driving this car would eventually get her spotted, it had also been her lifeline over the past couple of days. It had allowed them to get away at a moment's notice and put miles between themselves and danger. It was reliable, and she'd also thought that they could sleep in it, if need be.

With that thought, she turned her attention back to the cars on the forecourt. If she ran out of money there might come a time where they would be forced to sleep in the car. Because of that, her line of sight went straight to an old maroon red Ford Mondeo Estate. There was plenty of space in the back, and they could put down the rear seats and create enough room to make a bed for them both, if the worst came to the worst.

Behind her, the engine of her Nissan grumbled to life. She sucked in a breath, her shoulders tensed, praying she wouldn't also hear the crunch of tyres on gravel as he drove it away, laughing at her stupidity, but that didn't happen.

She approached the Ford Mondeo and peered through the window. The interior was tidy enough. She wondered how many miles were on the clock. She guessed it didn't really matter as long as it was reliable. The last thing she wanted was to break down on the side of the road. That would be a disaster.

The car salesman returned from checking her vehicle. "You interested in this one?"

"I think so," she said. "How many miles has it done?"

"Just over one hundred thousand, but it's an ex-company car, so it's been taken care of. All the services are up to date, and it passed its last MOT with flying colours."

She would be about eight grand down by doing the exchange, but that didn't matter.

She looked the man in the eye. "And you promise you won't file any paperwork for at least a few days?"

"How does a week sound?" he said. "Should give you enough time to get plenty far away from here."

"A week would be good."

How differently would things be in a week? Right now, she couldn't see an end to this, but one would have to come eventually. She would also have to drive uninsured which made her anxious but she couldn't risk filling in forms that would get her insured on the car.

He put his hand out to her. "In which case, you've got a deal."

She forced a smile and shook it.

"Let's go inside."

She followed him into the portacabin. Time was ticking by, and she was aware of how long she'd left Chloe for. Her daughter was most likely still asleep—happy to have the room to herself for an hour and not have to put up with her mother crashing around. She wished she could trust Chloe completely and know that she wouldn't do anything stupid like try to contact one of her friends back home, but one thing these last couple of days had proven was that as much as she loved Chloe, she couldn't always be trusted to make sensible decisions. She was sure she'd read somewhere that a teenager's brain hadn't developed enough yet to allow them to balance out choices and so they acted recklessly. She hoped it was just Chloe's age that she could blame and not have to feel as though there was something about her own child that she didn't like.

The portacabin was small and stuffy. She took a seat on the opposite side of the desk, and her hand trembled as she picked up the pen to sign the paperwork.

"All done," he said. "I hope everything works out for you, Mrs..."

"It's Miss. Miss Moore."

She instantly realised her mistake. She wasn't married. Never had been. Yet she'd claimed she was running from her abusive husband.

Her cheeks heated. "It's my maiden name," she blurted. "Never got round to changing it."

He shifted uncomfortably in his seat. "Right."

The walls seem to close in around her, and the air grew even thicker, cloying. A rush of heat spread through her body, and all she knew was that she needed to get out of there. What if she'd made him suspicious? What if he did decide to call the police and report her? But it was too late now—what was done was done.

She stood, her legs shaky.

"Wait, you've forgotten something," he said.

"Have I?"

He dangled a fob from his fingers. "The keys?"

"Gosh, yes, of course. Sorry, my head is all over the place."

"I understand."

He didn't, though. He didn't understand in the slightest.

"And you promise you'll stick to our agreement," she checked.

"I promise. I most likely wouldn't get around to sorting out my paperwork until then anyway."

She took the keys and left the portacabin, stepping out into unseasonably bright sunshine. Seeing her Nissan sitting there, and knowing it was no longer hers, brought tears to her eyes again. Her throat constricted with pain. How stupid to be getting upset over a car, but a stupid little part of her felt as though she was abandoning a family member.

She forced her attention towards her new vehicle. This was a good thing, she told herself. In the Mondeo, they had complete anonymity. No one would be looking for it. It was a step towards freedom, at least in the very short term.

Chapter Twenty-Two

It was now the third day since Tai Moore had been thrown from the Clifton Suspension Bridge, and Ryan didn't feel he was any closer to finding out who'd done it than he'd been on that first morning.

The investigation now seemed to be pulled in two directions. One part was trying to uncover what Tai Moore had been involved in during the days and weeks before she'd died, and the other was trying to work out where the Jenningses had disappeared to.

His phone rang on his desk, and he answered it. "DI Chase."

"Ryan, it's Isaac Madakor from digital forensics. I've completed the forensic imaging on the laptop belonging to Tai Moore. Got time for a chat?"

"Absolutely."

"Want to meet me over the road? I don't know about you, but I skipped breakfast."

Ryan didn't need to ask where he meant by 'over the road'. There was a local greasy spoon café that was frequented by members of the force, and they did a good run in bacon butties and all-day breakfasts.

"Sounds good to me."

He hadn't eaten anything before leaving Donna's that morning and he could do with a decent coffee as well.

THE CAFÉ WAS QUIET at this time of day, with the breakfast rush already over and the lunchtime madness not yet begun. The air was redolent with a strange combination of chip pan fat and coffee.

Ryan recognised a couple of other people from the office, nodding polite hellos to them, and then he found a table in a corner, away from everyone else. He didn't know yet what Isaac would have to tell him, but he didn't want it to be overheard. The table was covered in a wipeable cloth with metal clips holding the edges to the wood beneath. In the centre of the table sat a small vase with a bunch of fake flowers, and next to that was a pot containing sachets of sugar, salt, and various sauces.

A young waitress came over, gave him an awkward smile, and poised her pencil over her notepad. "You know what you're having?"

He considered waiting until Isaac was here and decided against it. In their job roles, things could change at a moment's notice. Either one of them could get a call to say they were needed elsewhere, and then he'd miss out on yet another meal.

He took a quick glance at the laminated menu. This wasn't the sort of place you came to if you were worried about your cholesterol.

"Coffee and a sausage sandwich, please."

"On white or brown?"

He didn't think brown bread was going to save his health at this point. "White is good, thanks."

She scribbled it down. "Be right back."

The café door opened, the bell above it chiming out, and Ryan recognised the person he was here to meet.

Isaac Madakor was in his late thirties. He was Nigerian-born but had been brought over to the UK by his parents when he'd only been young. He had the sort of brain Ryan couldn't understand. Anyone who worked in bits and bytes rather than words blew Ryan's mind. He just greyed out when anyone started talking technical. It was another language to him.

Ryan half rose as Isaac approached, and the two men shook hands. Isaac took a seat opposite.

He picked up the laminated menu. "What are you having?"

"Sausage sandwich and a coffee."

He grinned. "Michelin star stuff."

The waitress came back over with Ryan's coffee, and Isaac ordered for himself.

"So, what have you got for me?" Ryan asked.

Isaac launched straight in. "As I said on the phone, I've completed the forensic analysis of the murdered girl's laptop. It made for an interesting investigation, that's for sure."

That sounded promising.

"The first thing I did was put together an activity timeline to figure out what Tai Moore had been doing online in the days and weeks before her death. As I'm sure you're aware, everything she's done on the system has metadata file stamps."

Ryan lifted a hand to stop him. "Imagine you're explaining this to a child. A small child. My technical knowledge isn't up to much."

"Okay. Think of it like this. Every file on the system contains information. It can tell me who saved it and when. What was downloaded, what websites were visited. It essentially creates a timeline of activity. I try to only dig as far as is needed in an investigation, but in one like this where the next of kin has given consent so we're not guided by what's on a warrant, and where we don't really know what we're looking for except for something out of the ordinary, it's harder to know exactly where to dig. That's where coming up with a timeline helps. It allows us to see a bit more into the user's mindset."

"Okay. And what did you find?"

"Up until recently, it was easy to see what sort of websites she visited and searches she used. They were all the usual ones I'd expect to see of a teenage girl, though there was a high number of searches for things like 'how can I make money online' and 'how to manifest money.'"

Ryan nodded. "That aligns with what we know of Tai. It seems she had expensive taste. You said 'up until recently', so what changed?"

"This is where I had to dig deeper and things got interesting. She was using a normal browser right up until two months ago when she switched to something else."

"What?"

"She's been using a browser called Tor. Have you heard of it?"

"You can access the dark web on it, right?"

"That's right. It's where people go on the internet if they don't want anyone finding out who's been on there or what they've been going. It uses onions, or circuits, to hide their location."

Ryan took a sip of his coffee. It wasn't great, but it was distinctly better than the vending machine crap. "And a seventeen-year-old girl has been using it?"

"Yes. People believe that if they use Tor, the police can't track them. That's simply not true. We have our ways. Tai didn't turn off her JavaScript so we were able to see what she'd been doing. "

The waitress arrived back with their order and slid a plate of food in front of them both. "Can I get you anything else?"

"No, this is great, thanks." Ryan checked the small pot with all the sauce sachets for some brown sauce. He couldn't eat a sausage or bacon sarnie without brown sauce. He picked one out, opened up his sandwich, tore the corner of the sachet off with his teeth, and applied it liberally to the sausages. He put the lid back on the sandwich and picked it up and took a big bite.

Isaac had been doing something similar to his own food, and the men fell silent for a minute while they ate.

When Ryan had devoured most of his sandwich, he washed it down with another swig of coffee and jumped back into the conversation.

"So, what was Tai doing on Tor?"

Isaac finished with his sandwich, too. "People can use Tor to buy weapons or drugs, or even hire an assassin."

Ryan arched an eyebrow. "I assume Tai wasn't trying to hire a hitman."

"No, she wasn't. I was able to use her laptop to trace which websites she'd been visiting. There was one website in particular that came up." Isaac wiped his hands on a paper napkin, opened his laptop, and his fingers flew over the keys. He twisted the screen around so Ryan could see it.

www-dot-SearchingBenefits-dot-com

"What is that? Some kind of dating site?"

Isaac nodded. "A very specific dating site. It's being touted as a sugar babies site."

Ryan blinked. "Sugar babies? I've heard of a sugar daddy, but *baby*?"

"Yeah, it's what they call the young women the men want to date, only, in this case, it's very young women."

Ryan thought to how old Tai had been. "Like seventeen year olds?"

"And sixteen year olds, by the look of it."

Isaac pointed at the dropdown box of the website that allowed the user to scroll through the potential 'dates' they could use the website to organise. Ryan pulled the laptop closer so no one would be able to look over his shoulder and went through them. They all had usernames rather than their real names, and the photographs they'd used either had the faces blurred out, or else the images were cropped. While the photographs weren't explicit in any way, they certainly didn't leave much to the imagination. It was clear what was on offer. There was nothing much in the bios that said anything much about the personalities of the girls, it was all about what they were like physically. Blonde hair, blue eyes, one hundred and ten pounds, D-sized bra cup. It was like reading a shopping list. Oh, and not to forget the girls' ages, too. There was no one on the site over twenty years old, and most were in their late teens.

"Most online dating websites expect their users to be eighteen when they join," Isaac said. "The fact this site clearly doesn't request such a thing is probably why it's on the dark web as opposed to a mainstream search engine. There are other teen dating sites online, but the cutoff age for using them is nineteen. If you go through the male users on this site, you'll see that basically none of them are the same age as the girls. The youngest are in their late twenties and thirties, but the ages of the men go right up to their sixties."

Ryan screwed up his face in disgust. "A sixty-year-old man should have no interest in a seventeen-year-old girl."

"My thoughts exactly, but, in this country, once a person has turned sixteen, it's not illegal for someone to have sex with them, no matter how old they are. To me, it's borderline paedophilia, but that's only morally, not legally. If all these girls are sixteen and over, they're not breaking the law by offering up a dating site to them. The men would argue that there's nothing wrong with being attracted to young, beautiful women either."

"They're not women, they're girls," Ryan said.

"I'm still playing devil's advocate, but not in the eyes of the law."

Ryan shook his head. "But to sell those services online? I mean, it's clear there's only one thing these men are interested in. In their bios, they're not mentioning any long-term connections, or talking about what kind of relationship they're after, or even what their interests are. Surely, sixteen and seventeen year olds aren't allowed to sell sex online."

"The owners of the website would say that they're not selling anything. It's simply a dating site. What happens between two people outside of the site is nothing to do with them."

"Then why do they need to be using a dark web browser?

"They'd argue it was to keep their users' anonymity. These kinds of companies tend to be fiercely protective of their users' info. We could try for a warrant, but they'd fight it in court while dumping the data."

"Shit." Ryan thought for a moment. "What about payments made via the website. Would we be able to track those?"

Isaac pursed his lips. "Unlikely. The payments are anonymous, too, using bitcoin, however, some people have their bitcoin linked to their PayPal accounts, so that might give us a few options. I'd have to dig deeper."

"I'm going to need you to dig deeper then. There's a seventeen-year-old girl dead and a possibility one of the men she met via this website was the person responsible for killing her."

He sat back, the coffee and sausage sandwich suddenly churning in his stomach, acid burning up his throat. So, this was where Tai had been getting her extra money from. It had nothing to do with drugs, which meant Richard Foyle might not have had anything to do with her death either.

"I can go through the usernames of each of the men on there as well," Isaac offered. "Plenty of people use the same username for multiple sites or even have email addresses or Google accounts connected to them. It would be good to narrow things down a bit, as obviously that's a huge undertaking considering the number of men who subscribe to this site."

"How many men subscribe?" Ryan asked.

"Hundreds."

"Dammit." Ryan thought for a moment. "I assume you tried to find Tai Moore on the site?"

"Yes. I searched using any of the usernames I'd found her using on various different sites, plus I searched using her description. We know how tall she is and how much she weighs from her post-mortem, plus her age, hair and eye colour."

"Nothing?" Ryan asked.

"Nothing. But that doesn't mean she wasn't on here. The amount of time she spent on this site tells me she was."

"Plus we know she had extra money. We found lots of expensive makeup, clothes, and jewellery in her room. If she'd deleted her account, that would mean she'd have deleted any messages she might have received from her killer as well?"

"Yes, although there's a good chance they'd have moved their messages onto another platform. Though if it was something like Snapchat, those messages delete almost instantly, so they wouldn't have left a trace."

"We don't have her phone anyway." Ryan rubbed his hand over his face. He hoped this wasn't going to be a dead end. They needed something substantial on this case, and every time he thought they were getting somewhere, the lead disintegrated like sand through his fingers. Then he thought of something. "There's a second girl, Chloe Jennings. Can you do a search on her. She's five feet seven, about a hundred and twenty pounds, blonde hair, blue eyes. Seventeen years old."

Isaac turned the laptop back around to face him and got to work.

A few minutes passed, and then he said, "There are a couple of different possibilities. Take a look."

Ryan pulled the laptop back again. He scrolled through the profiles, scanning each one with an eye for detail. With the heads cut off, it was difficult to know for sure. He used his phone to bring up the social media profiles for Chloe Jennings. There still hadn't been any updates. He could be wrong, and this wasn't the connection between Tai and Chloe, outside of their schooling, but his gut told him he wasn't.

He went through every photograph on her social media, trying to imprint every detail so he could use it to match up to the profiles on the sugar baby website. There was a good chance Chloe had also deleted her profile, in which case this attempt to narrow things down would be fruitless, but he had to try.

He stiffened, his gaze locking on to something. "Do you see this?" He passed the laptop back over to Isaac. "She has a mole on the inside of her wrist, right where her hand becomes her arm."

"Yeah, I see it."

In the photograph, Chloe was smiling and pushing her hair back from her face, so her hand and arm were lifted, revealing the mole.

"If we can find a girl with the same mole from the bio pictures, I'd say we're onto the right person."

Isaac frowned. "What's her connection with the murdered girl?"

Ryan filled him in. "They were friends at school. She's missing now, together with her mother. They vanished around the same time Tai was killed."

"You think they've run? Or that someone took them?"

"Their car is missing, so my instinct says they've run. They left phones and laptops behind, which might mean they went in a hurry, or else they deliberately left them in order not to be traced. What they're running from, though, I'm not so sure."

"You think it might have some connection to this site?" Isaac asked.

"I think it's a possibility, yes. If Tai was on here and whoever she got involved with ended up killing her, then there's a possibility that Chloe is involved with the same person as well. Maybe that's why they took off. They might have been running from him."

"But why not just come straight to the police. If they had an idea who killed Tai, why not come and tell the police so we can arrest them?"

"I'm not sure. Perhaps they're scared. People don't always think straight when they're frightened."

"Let's try and find her then."

Together, they continued to scroll through the girls' bios and pictures.

"What about this one?" Isaac pointed at the screen.

Ryan had to squint. "Can you enlarge the image at all?"

"Of course." Isaac blew it up. "How's that?"

The small mole was in the same place as the photographs on Chloe Jennings' social media.

"I think that's our girl. Good work. Can you get into her message board at all?"

"I can try. It might involve me having to create a profile for myself. Even if I can't see the messages, there's a chance I'll be able to see what usernames have been messaging her."

"That'll help narrow things down, won't it?"

"Definitely. Leave it with me and I'll see what I can find."

"Thanks, Isaac."

"There's something else you should know about that I found on the laptop. There are numerous deleted photographs. The photographs are...suggestive in nature. Most of them don't include her face."

Ryan shook his head. "Jesus. Do you think she's used the photographs for the website?"

"Or she's sending them to someone privately."

"Is there any way to find out who she might have sent them to?" Ryan asked.

"I suspect they've been either sent via the website or she's moved them onto her phone and sent via one of the social media apps."

Ryan huffed out air. "Damn. We really need to find that phone."

"It would definitely help."

Isaac reached into his pocket for his wallet, but Ryan waved him down. "Nah, it's on me."

"You sure?"

"If I can't afford to buy someone lunch, I think I'd have to go to my boss for a pay rise."

Isaac chuckled. "Thanks. I'll get you next time."

"You can repay me by finding out which creep has been paying for the company of teenage girls, and possibly murdering them."

"I'll do my best."

They shook hands, and Isaac put his laptop away and left the café. Ryan paid the bill, including a generous tip for the waitress.

He needed to update his team with the information about the sugar babies site. Was Chloe Jennings and her mother in danger from whoever had killed Tai?

Chapter Twenty-Three

R yan went back to the office to fill his team in.
This was a huge turning point in the investigation.
They now had a possible motive behind Tai's murder, but there
was also a second girl out there who might be in danger.

In the incident room, he addressed his team.

"I'd say this information puts Richard Foyle and Lorraine
Moore in the clear. Our biggest leads are Chloe Jennings and
the website, *www-dot-SearchingBenefits-dot-com*. Tai Moore
must have made contact with someone who wanted to do more
than just date a teenage girl. He wanted to murder her, too.
Since Chloe Jennings is also missing, but with her mother, I'd
say they've run out of fear the same thing will happen to her.
We need to find Chloe before this man does.

"We found numerous deleted suggestive photographs on
Tai's laptop, which means she might have been using either
the website or possibly a different app to send them to this
person. If they moved their conversation off the website, they
might have been using an app on Tai's phone, which means
we need to prioritise finding it. We got a ping off it near the
bridge around eleven the night before her body was found, so
it makes sense that she had it on her when she was killed. So
either someone took it, or we just haven't found it yet.

"The search teams are still working on it, but it's not easy
terrain. We've needed to get climbers in, and, if nothing shows

up soon, we'll have to get divers in as well. There's always the possibility that there's nothing to find and whoever killed her took her phone to hide their tracks."

Ryan took a moment to make sure everyone was following him. He didn't want to see them distracted or checking their phones, but all eyes were trained on him.

"We need to try again with the warrant to search the Jennings' house. Now we know what we're looking for if we do a search of the property—any connections Chloe Jennings might have had with the website—we're more likely to be granted it. I also need someone to find out who owns this website and contact them directly, and see what information we can get out of them, though I suspect it's going to take too much time to be of any use."

It was an avenue he couldn't ignore, however.

"I can do that, boss," Craig volunteered.

"Good. Who is working on the missing time between her leaving the house and getting to the bridge at eleven? That's four hours. She ate a burger? Did she meet someone? Could it have been the same person she met through the website, the same one who potentially killed her?"

"I'm on it," Dev said. "I've still got a lot of CCTV footage to go through."

Ryan looked to the two female members of his team. "Linda and Shonda, can I put you onto finding the Jenningses. Run the licence plate for the car, talk to friends and family, see if there's anywhere they might have gone. We need to request their bank records, too. If either of them have used a bank card in the last few days, it'll give us an idea about what direction they've headed in."

Both women nodded.

"We've got a lot to do," Ryan continued, "but we're getting somewhere, I can feel it."

He left his team to get on with their work and filled in DCI Hirst with the progress that had been made that morning. It was true what he'd said to his team about feeling like they were finally making inroads into finding out who'd killed Tai. Some sick predator who had a thing for teenage girls. The only thing that didn't make complete sense to him was that Tai didn't have any signs of either sexual assault or activity on her body. Sex was clearly a motive for whoever had contacted her, considering the explicit nature of the photographs. Unless he was one of these men who thought that girls who used their sexuality to make money should be punished, and he'd done that by throwing Tai Moore off a bridge.

Ryan left Hirst's office to return to his desk. He stretched his back out, lifting his arms above his head, wincing at the creak in his shoulders and spine. Christ, he felt like he was getting old, and he wasn't even fifty yet. Pretty soon, he was going to start injuring himself by doing things like sleeping wrong or checking the blind spot in the car the wrong way.

He glanced up as DC Penn approached. The younger officer's expression was tense, and he was wringing his hands in front of him. Clearly, something was wrong.

That was the thing about being in his job role. It wasn't just that he had multiple cases on his plate at one time and had to figure out how to juggle investigations between court times and everything else, he also had to manage all the people on his team. When they had personal things come up, they needed to be dealt with. Time off had to be allocated, and if it was something that might affect how they worked, that needed to be handled, too. This wasn't a job you could just leave at home. It impacted every part of your life. And the same was true the other way around, too. A police officer's homelife affected what kind of copper they made.

"Craig, what's up?"

"I'm really sorry to do this to you, but I've got a family emergency."

Ryan frowned. "What kind of emergency?"

"My mother's had a stroke. She's in hospital."

Ryan tried to remember what he knew about Penn's family. "She doesn't live nearby, does she?"

He shook his head. "No, she's up north. Doncaster. I have to go and see her. It's not looking good."

"Yes, of course. We can manage without you. Family always comes first. Is there anything we can do to help?"

"No, but I appreciate the offer. I'm sorry, but I don't know how long I'm going to be. Could be a couple of days, but might be longer, depending on...what happens."

"I understand. Just keep me informed, okay? You've got my mobile number. If you don't feel you can talk, ping me a text."

Craig nodded. "Thanks for being so understanding."

"Hey, it's your mother. We only get one of them, right?"

"Right."

It wasn't great that they were going to be one man down right in the middle of an important case. He'd have to talk to his DCI if they started to flounder and see if she could pull in some more resources from other teams.

Dev Kharral called out across the office floor, "Boss, we've got a hit on some CCTV footage the evening Tai went missing."

"Excellent. Where?"

"A McDonald's in town. Come and see."

Ryan rose from his chair and crossed the office floor to drag one up to Dev's desk.

Dev spoke quickly, clearly excited by this new development. "We knew from her stomach contents that she'd eaten something with ground beef and bread, most likely a burger. Her mother said she hadn't eaten before she went out, so it stands to reason that she grabbed something that evening. Bearing in mind that she's seventeen, I took the chance that she's more likely to go to a popular takeaway than have a sit-down meal somewhere. The most popular place with teenagers is the good old Golden Arches." He pulled up a map. "We know that Tai left her home here in Brislington at ten minutes past seven in the evening. She was on foot and walked towards the city centre. We caught her on several CCTV cameras on the way, but then we lose her before she reaches the city centre."

"Okay," Ryan said, following along.

Dev clicked to a screen with another map, but this one had places marked out on it. "There are four MacDonald's restaurants between her home and Clifton. I requested the CCTV footage from each of them for the evening Tai was killed. Taking into account that it would have taken her at least forty minutes to get from her home into the city centre and the same again to get from the city centre to the bridge, I checked the times between eight p.m. and ten. I could have gone slightly later, but I reasoned that she would have needed time to buy her meal and eat it before she set off for Clifton."

Ryan nodded in agreement. "Makes sense. So what did you find."

He pulled up another screen on his computer. The image was blurry, but it was clear it was Tai standing in line, waiting to order.

"This was taken at eight-fifteen the evening she died."

It was a weekday evening, so while it wasn't completely dead in there, it was quiet. Tai didn't have to wait long before the queue moved forwards and she ordered her food.

"Is she there alone?" Ryan asked.

"For the moment, yes, but then she finds a table, waits for about ten minutes, and someone else shows up."

Ryan leaned in closer. "Have you got footage of that?"

"It's not a great angle, but look."

Dev clicked to a different shot, clearly taken from a different angle. It was the back of Tai's head, but she was easily recognisable with her tight black curls. Someone approached her, and Tai got to her feet, and the two people embraced.

"You recognise who that is?" Dev asked.

Ryan nodded. "That's Chloe Jennings. The girl who is currently missing with her mother. Was she the last person to see Tai alive?"

"Possibly, but we can't know for sure. Chloe left Tai at the table for a few minutes while she went and ordered her own meal, and then the two of them sit together for what feels like forever but ends up being just shy of an hour. I called and spoke to the manager there, and he said it's pretty normal for teens to come in and order one small fries between them and then hang out for hours. They treat it like a bit of a drop-in centre."

"Did anyone working there that night happen to overhear what they were talking about?"

He shook his head. "Not that I've found so far, but this is new information, and we need to get some officers down to interview the people working that night. They are interrupted a couple of times, though." He fast-forwarded the CCTV footage. "At eight-forty, two young men go up to the girls and speak to them. It's not for long, literally a matter of minutes. It's unclear if they know each other or not, or if the men are just trying to pick them up."

"Have we managed to track down the identities of the men yet? Could they know the girls from the sugar baby site?"

"Not yet," Dev said. "They paid with cash at the counter, and as you can see, the footage and the angle of the camera isn't good. We've just got a glimpse of one of their faces and the back of the head of the other."

Ryan wondered if either of these men had arranged to meet the girls through the website. They didn't seem old enough, but it wasn't as though he'd gone through the profiles of every single man on the site yet. He had Isaac doing that. While they'd all seemed older, there was no reason why they couldn't have lied about their ages.

"Could they have been waiting for the girls when they left?" Ryan asked. "Maybe they arranged to meet them later? One might have had a car and they drove Tai up to the bridge."

"But then what happened to Chloe?"

Ryan rubbed his finger across his lips as he tried to put together the possible scenario that would end with one girl dead and another on the run.

"Could Tai have escaped? Maybe the men said they were going to give the girls a lift somewhere and then tried to take them in a different direction, and Tai managed to get away. She could have been waiting on the bridge for someone to pick her up, and one of the men found her again and pushed her off?"

"Or maybe Chloe was the one who escaped," Dev suggested. "The men took Tai to the bridge."

Ryan's mind whirred, picking up all the different possibilities, trying to see Tai's final moments through her eyes. It was all speculation at the moment, but if he didn't act out every possibility in his mind, he thought he would miss something.

"Why would they have just left her there until one of them decided to throw her off? It doesn't fit. Besides, wouldn't Tai have called someone for help if she'd been abducted and run away?"

"She did call someone," Dev said. "She called Chloe just after ten, remember, which means the girls weren't together then."

Ryan frowned. "She waited on the bridge for twelve minutes. Does that strike you as the actions of someone who is scared and running? And doesn't she approach the person who pushes her, like she knows them? She wouldn't do that if it was someone she was fearful of."

"I agree. There's something else I still haven't shown you."

"Go on." Ryan turned his attention back to the screen.

Dev hit fast-forward on the footage. "Watch from here."

The two girls were alone again, except this time, their conversation was more animated. Both girls gestured with their hands as they spoke, and they leaned in closer over the table, their heads not quite touching, but not far from it.

"Are they whispering?" Ryan wondered. "Is that why they're leaning together, so no one will hear what they're saying?"

"The way they're moving their hands, they seem like they should be shouting," Dev said.

"But no one in the restaurant noticed the two of them fighting. Check out the rest of the shot."

A number of tables were filled with people, but no one glanced in the direction of the two girls. If they'd been shouting at each other, with their faces up close like that, everyone would have been looking.

Suddenly, Tai shot out of her seat, glared at Chloe, grabbed her phone off the table, and left.

Ryan would have given anything to be a fly on the wall at that conversation. He'd put any amount of money on the argument being around the sugar babies website. Had Tai been the one to get Chloe into it, or the other way around? People they went to college with said that Tai was a queen bee, so did that make her more influential than Chloe? Not necessarily. They didn't really know enough about Chloe yet, since they'd aimed most of their focus at Tai. Tai must have deleted her account by this point. Had she been trying to convince Chloe to do the same, only Chloe had refused? Why had that upset Tai so much? What about the two young men who had approached them? Did they know the girls? Did they have something to do with Tai's death and Chloe going missing?

"So not only was Chloe possibly the last person to see Tai alive, they also fought the night Tai died. Was that why Tai called Chloe? Was it to apologise?"

Dev glanced over at him. "You don't think Chloe had anything to do with her death?"

"I'd say it's unlikely. We need to be able to rule those two men out of the investigation, though. If they're not involved, it muddies the water."

"Agreed. I can do an appeal on social media, see if anyone recognises them?"

"Yes, do that." Ryan thought for a moment. "What time is it when Tai storms out?"

"Nine twenty-eight, but she doesn't reach the bridge until after eleven. Even if she'd walked really slowly, she'd still have an hour to spare, so what's she doing in that time?"

"I assume you've tried to track her progress through the city when she leaves?"

"Yes, but I haven't got anywhere. She might have got in a car, or even a bus. But if she did, I haven't found the CCTV footage for it yet."

Ryan sat back. "You did well tracking down the McDonald's footage. If we needed more proof that Chloe is involved in Tai's case, we have it now. Both Chloe and Faye Jennings need to be officially registered as missing persons, so can you contact someone over at misper? If we can track them down, we'll be one step closer to finding out who killed Tai Moore."

Chapter Twenty-Four

Mallory had been considering taking a break for lunch when her phone rang and the number for Helping Hands flashed up.

What now?

Sometimes it felt like she was constantly battling fires. What she needed was a holiday, though she didn't do beach holidays. She'd like to go to Canada, or maybe somewhere in Northern Europe, and hike into the wilderness, and stay in a log cabin somewhere that had no internet access or even phone reception.

Of course, she knew she'd never actually do that. She'd worry the whole time about Oliver and how her family were coping without her.

Maybe she could take him with her one day, though Oliver didn't like change. He was always more relaxed with routine and the comforts of home.

She answered the call. "Mallory speaking."

"Oh, Mallory, it's Diana from Helping Hands."

"Hello, Diana."

"I'm afraid I've sent Daniel's replacement over to your house today, but we're having a bit of an issue."

"What kind of an issue?"

"Oliver won't let her into the house. He's asking for Daniel."

Damn it. One thing Oliver could be was stubborn. Once he'd made his mind up about something, it was very difficult to change it again.

"Tell her to go home. We'll manage without her. I'm sorry for wasting her time."

"Are you sure?"

"Yes, I'm sure. Oliver will be fine on his own. He's very independent. It was just good for him to have the company with Daniel."

"He and Daniel got on very well, didn't they? What a shame things didn't work out."

Guilt swathed itself around her. "Yes, it is a shame. I'll speak to Ollie, okay?"

"Whatever you think is best."

She ended the call and groaned. What was she supposed to do? Was she being selfish? Was she overreacting? Should she ask Daniel to come back and just put some provisions in place to make sure he was always gone by the time she got home? But the thought of having him in the house when she wasn't there made her uneasy, too.

Oliver was just going to have to adapt.

"Everything all right?" Ryan asked.

"Yeah, just some issues with this new person who's supposed to be helping Oliver." She paused and bit her lower lip. "You okay if I nip home for an hour, just to make sure he's okay?"

"Go for it. You won't be able to concentrate on your job if you're worrying about your brother."

Ryan had a point.

She grabbed her suit jacket. "Thanks, boss. I'll be back asap."

He nodded. "Say hi to Oliver from me."

MALLORY USED HER KEY to open the front door. "Oliver?"

She found him in his room, sitting on his bed, with his knees pulled up to his chest.

"Hi, Ollie." She perched on the edge of the bed. "Everything all right?"

"No. I want Daniel to come back. We never even finished my last puzzle."

She exhaled the air from her lungs. "We talked about this, bud. Daniel was...making me uncomfortable."

"He wasn't making me uncomfortable, though. He was my friend."

She blinked back tears. "I know. I'm so sorry things didn't work out."

They sat in silence for a moment, and Mallory tried to think of a way she could make Oliver understand.

"Do you remember that friend I had at school?" she said eventually. "Monique?"

"I think so. She had red hair?"

"That's right. The two of us were pretty close when we were teenagers. I wouldn't say she was my best friend, but she wasn't far off it. But then one day I overheard her saying mean things about you to one of our other friends, and so I decided I couldn't be friends with her anymore."

"I dunno why you're telling me this, Mallory." He sniffed.

"Because you and I stick together, right? And if one of us has a friend who is mean to the other one, we don't then still be friends with the person."

His eyes widened. "Daniel said mean things to you?"

"He wasn't very nice to me," she admitted.

Oliver took her hand. "I'm your brother, Mallory. I'll look after you. I won't be friends with someone who says mean things to you."

She pulled him in for a hug. "Thanks, Ollie. I won't be friends with anyone who says mean things about you either." They parted, and she looked into his eyes. "Now, will you at least consider giving someone else from Helping Hands a chance? They might be able to help you finish the puzzle."

"Maybe. I'll think about it."

"Thank you. Now, I have to get back to work. Are you going to be okay?"

"I'll be okay."

"Good."

As she left the house and headed back to her car, she caught a dart of movement across the road. She froze, her car keys in hand. Had someone been standing over the other side of the street, watching the house?

This was Bristol, it was a city. There were always people around. She was just letting her imagination run away with her. But then why did her skin prickle and her heart rate trip like that? She wasn't someone who normally gave in to flights of fancy.

Mallory reminded herself who she was and straightened her shoulders. She broke into a trot and crossed the road, heading in the direction the person had gone. She just wanted to put her mind at ease.

She rounded the corner and stopped. A woman pushing a pram headed towards her. Across the street, a couple in their eighties climbed out of a taxi. A man in a suit walked briskly, his phone clamped to his ear.

None of them were the person she'd thought she'd seen.

She took out her ID and held it open for the woman with the pram to see. "Excuse me, did you see a man with brown hair, in his late twenties to early thirties, walking this way just now?"

She shook her head. "No, sorry, but I wasn't paying much attention."

"Okay, thanks."

She must have imagined it.

Mallory turned and headed back to her car. She had work to do.

Chapter Twenty-Five

"I don't like this car," Chloe complained. "The engine is too loud, and it smells weird."

Faye sighed. "I preferred our car, too, but you know why we couldn't keep driving it."

Chloe slid down in her seat. "Can we at least find somewhere to stay for a few days now, instead of having to pack our stuff and leave again every morning. And can we buy new phones? Surely we can just get a couple of pay-as-you-go phones so we can browse the internet?"

"I don't trust you, Chloe. If you get a phone, you won't be able to help yourself. You'll get online and get in touch with your friends, or you'll log in to one of your social media accounts. I know you will."

"I won't, I promise!"

Faye shook her head. "I'm sorry, Chloe, but I can't trust you anymore. You know why."

Chloe threw her hands up. "Am I supposed to spend the rest of my life with no access to the internet? How do you think that's going to work? I'm almost eighteen years old. It's not as though you can stop me when I'm an adult."

"Yes, but right now, you're not an adult, are you? You're still under my care, and you've proven that I can't trust you. You lied to me. You lied so many times I've lost count. When I asked you where all the extra money came from, and the clothes, and the makeup, and you told me you were out babysitting or that one of your friends bought something but decided they didn't like it, and gave it to you, you lied to me. I can't believe I was such an idiot for believing you. I mean, I did consider the possibility that you might have been shoplifting, but I never—not for one second—thought you were capable of selling yourself like that."

"I said I was sorry," Chloe muttered, her face pale, her arms hugged around her chest.

"Sorry? You think sorry is going to cut it? I don't think so, Chloe. Not after what you did."

Chloe turned her face and wiped away a tear.

Was she being too hard on her daughter? Maybe, but then she thought that if she'd been harder to start with they'd never have ended up in this position, with nothing to their name but a few crappy clothes and an even crappier car.

Still, she couldn't help the wave of guilt that swept through her.

Faye remembered the sweet, loving girl Chloe had once been. She remembered how at the age of eleven or twelve, Chloe had insisted she would never drink or smoke or wear lots of makeup. She had to remind herself that Chloe had been manipulated. What Chloe had done wasn't the actions of the Chloe that Faye knew and loved. She'd been coerced by her so-called friend and groomed by older men. She was too easily influenced.

"I just hate this," Chloe said.

Faye slammed on the brakes, bringing the car to a squealing halt in the middle of the country lane. She was lucky there was no one behind her.

"Do you want to go back, Chloe? Is that it? Because we can turn around and go home right now, if that's really what you want. We can face up to everything and suffer the consequences."

Her daughter paled. "That wasn't what I was saying..."

"Wasn't it? Because that's how it felt to me. I'm not responsible for this situation...or maybe I am. Maybe I should have parented you better. I mean, I must have done something wrong for us to have ended up like this."

"But if I go back..."

Chloe's blue eyes filled with fresh tears.

Faye knew that was never going to happen. It didn't matter what threats she made, she'd never put either of them at risk like that. It didn't matter what had happened.

Faye sighed. "I wish you'd never got involved with that girl. She was bad news right from the start."

Chloe shook her head. "It wasn't her fault, Mum. She was no different to me. She just got mixed up with the wrong people."

"And then she dragged you down with her."

"She's dead, Mum! She's never coming back. So what use is it talking shit about her now?"

Faye closed her eyes briefly. "You're right, I'm sorry."

A car drove up behind them and beeped its horn. Faye put the car back into gear and got moving again.

Guilt at how harsh she'd been with her daughter filled her. "Look, how about we find somewhere to stop for a few days, just hang out, okay? We're in a different car now, and we've travelled a long way, so maybe we can afford to get off the road for a little while."

Chloe sniffed. "Okay, thanks, Mum. That would be good."

They'd hunker down for a while. Maybe the police would point the finger at someone, and then they'd be able to return. They could make up a story about them needing a break.

Or maybe she was telling herself lies and they'd never be able to go back.

Chapter Twenty-Six

Ryan took five minutes to look up the hospital where Craig's mother was and ordered some flowers for Mrs Penn. It was important for his team members to know they were being thought of and supported, even when they weren't in the office.

He'd just hit 'order' on the website when Linda approached.

"We've had a hit on Faye Jennings' car registration," she told Ryan.

He glanced up at her from his desk. "Where?"

"It's been sold to a small dealership just across the Scottish border near a town called Dornock. I've asked local police to go and pay the owner of the dealership a visit, see what he can tell us about the person who sold it to them."

"Wouldn't that person be Faye Jennings?" Ryan said.

Linda nodded. "Most likely, yes, but until we've spoken to him, we don't know that for sure, and it's best not to assume these things."

"You're right. What are they doing in Scotland?"

"My guess is that they're trying to put as much distance between them and Bristol as possible."

"It'll be good to find out if the mother and daughter have anyone else with them, too. They might have been taken by whoever killed Tai."

"It's a possibility."

Ryan bit the inside of his cheek as he thought. "Getting rid of the car was smart. We're not going to be able to use their car registration to find them now."

"Not that smart," she said. "While the car was sold to them, they did so in exchange for one already on the forecourt. The owner of the dealership can give us the registration of the Ford Mondeo they exchanged their car for."

"Good work."

Certainty that it was only a matter of time before they found the mother and daughter solidified inside him. The question was, when they did track them down, would Chloe Jennings be able to tell him exactly who had killed her friend?

Mallory stood and got his attention.

"Boss, we've got the warrant through to search the Jennings' house."

"Excellent. Looks like we've got work to do."

"Also," Mallory said, "misper contacted Faye Jennings' parents first thing this morning, and they're on their way up from Cornwall. Obviously, they're both extremely distressed that both their daughter and granddaughter are missing, and they're in their seventies, so let's go easy on them when they arrive."

"They're coming to the house?" he checked.

"As far as I'm aware. They might be of help to us."

"Good point. Let's get down there then."

A RESPONSE CAR WAS parked outside the Jennings' house, a uniformed officer positioned at the front door to prevent anyone else coming inside.

Ryan had the search warrant case containing gloves, protective shoe covers, evidence bags of all sizes, and a camera. He opened it up, and he and Mallory put on gloves and footwear.

"Let's take this methodically," Ryan said. "Start on the left-hand side of the room and work counterclockwise. We're looking for anything that might connect Chloe Jennings with either Tai Moore or the sugar babies website. We already know from the welfare check that they've left their phones and laptops here, so they're of priority to seize. That doesn't mean we won't find a hidden phone or tablet, though, so keep your eyes peeled."

They started the search, working carefully. This was part of the job Ryan enjoyed. His nature meant he was methodical with an eye for detail. He had his routine way of carrying out searches, ensuring not an inch of space was missed. If there was something to find, he would find it.

It didn't take them long to locate the phones and laptops.

Ryan bagged them. "Let's get them sent over to digital forensics. If Isaac Madakor can work his magic on them, he might be able to work out who it is connecting Chloe and Tai."

Chloe's phone could be of particular importance. If there was a contact on it who she'd sent the same sort of photos that they'd found on Tai's computer, it might lead them straight to their culprit.

Voices came from outside the front door, together with a scuffle of activity.

A couple in their seventies, both wearing matching expressions of concern, stood outside, peering anxiously through the open front door at the police activity.

"This is Mr and Mrs Jennings, Faye's parents," the officer said.

Mrs Jennings wrung her hands. "We're so worried about Faye and Chloe. We drove up as soon as we got the call."

"It's okay," Ryan said, "you can let them through."

They'd finished the search, and this wasn't a crime scene, as far as they were aware, and Faye's parents could be of help to them.

He took off his gloves and put his hand out to shake first Faye's mother's hand and then her father's. "I'm DI Chase. Thank you for coming. I hope you'll be able to help us track down your daughter and granddaughter."

"They're not in any trouble, are they?" Mr Jennings asked.

"We don't believe so, no. We're just concerned that they've not made contact with their places of work or college and that no one has heard from them."

There was no reason to go into any detail with them right now.

"I'd tried phoning her," Mrs Jennings said, "but the call just went through to her answerphone."

"We found her phone here, and it was switched off." Ryan continued, "I'm hoping you'll be able to give us some idea about what might have happened. Would you be able to check and let us know if anything obvious is missing. Any suitcases or bags? Any of their favourite clothing or shoes? If they packed a bag before they left, then it means they're more likely to just be away somewhere."

Mrs Jennings glanced anxiously at her husband. "I don't think Chloe's passport is up to date. Faye was complaining about the cost of getting it renewed."

Mr Jennings nodded. "Yes, that's right."

Ryan offered them both a smile. "Okay, that's good. It means they won't have gone far."

Mrs Jennings chewed on her lower lip. "I hope not. Why on earth would they just leave like this?"

"That's what we're trying to find out. When did you last speak to your daughter or granddaughter?"

"Only a few days ago. Faye called me on the Sunday, just like she normally does."

"Did she give you the impression anything was wrong?"

"No, not at all. She was perfectly fine."

"What about Chloe?"

She shook her head. "I'm not really sure. We've exchanged a few messages, but I can't remember when I last spoke to her. You know what teenagers can be like. They only want to spend time with their friends, not their boring old grandparents."

"I'm sure you're neither boring nor old."

"Days like this I feel old, DI Chase."

He gestured to the rest of the house. "If you could take a look around, we'd appreciate it."

The couple did as he'd asked, moving slowly through the rooms, checking their family's possessions. Both Ryan and Mallory kept an eye on them, making sure there was no chance of them pocketing anything they might not want the police to see. Ryan doubted that would happen—they didn't seem the type—plus, he and Mallory had already been over the place.

When they'd finished, they turned back to the two detectives.

"I think a couple of their cases are missing, and their toothbrushes aren't in the bathroom," Mrs Jennings said. "Also, Chloe has a stuffed bear with a heart on it that she's had since she was a child, and that's missing, too."

Tears swam in her eyes and trickled down her lined cheeks.

Ryan felt for her. "I'm sorry this is so upsetting for you, Mrs Jennings. We really are doing everything we can to track them down. Do you know if they have any connections with anyone in Scotland?"

She blinked. "Scotland? No, not that I'm aware of. Why do you ask?"

"We believe Faye's car has been spotted there, that's all."

Hope appeared in her eyes. "So maybe they have just gone on holiday and didn't tell anyone."

She clearly wanted to give herself a reason not to worry.

"It's a possibility, yes." He didn't add that it was highly unlikely that they'd go on holiday and sell their vehicle, or that people didn't normally go away without taking their phones with them.

"There's no sign of Faye's handbag either," Mrs Jennings added.

"That's good. Sounds like they left of their own free will then." Or someone had forced their hand and they'd simply had enough time to pack.

"Are you planning on staying somewhere local?" Ryan asked.

"We were going to stay here, if that's okay," Mr Jennings said. "We have a spare key."

"That's fine. It'll be good to have someone here in case they decide to return home. You'll be able to be the first ones to let us know."

The couple glanced at each other with small, reassuring smiles, as though they were telling themselves everything would be okay.

Ryan hoped it would be.

He checked his watch. The day had slipped by, and he had arranged to go to the house to have dinner with Donna again that evening. He hoped he wasn't going to have to cancel, though of course, he would if they found Chloe and Faye Jennings.

Chapter Twenty-Seven

It had been another long day, and Mallory was relieved to be going home. She wondered about Faye and Chloe Jennings and what had kept them away from their own home. Was Faye trying to protect her daughter from whatever—and whoever—had killed Tai Moore?

What extremes would a mother go to in order to protect her child?

She climbed out of her car and headed to the front door. No lights were on inside. Oliver was out at a club—one of his social clubs, not the music kind. He was meeting with other young people who had Downs Syndrome. There had even been some couples emerge out of the group, which was lovely. The thought of Oliver having a relationship one day and for Oliver and his girlfriend to live as an independent couple would be amazing in Mallory's mind. She just hoped he didn't get his heart broken along the way.

She fished into her bag for her keys, located them, and opened the front door. Sudden footsteps came behind her, and she spun around, but not quickly enough. Hands grabbed her shoulders and shoved her across her doorstep and into her house. She almost fell, half-tripping over her own feet, but somehow managed to stay upright.

She knew who it was before she'd even had the chance to catch sight of him.

Daniel.

She was strong and trained, but she hadn't been prepared. He entered the house right behind her and slammed the front door shut, closing them off from the rest of the world.

Mallory spun to face him. "What the fuck are you doing, Daniel? You know I'm a police officer, right?"

He narrowed his eyes and folded his arms across his chest. "So you keep telling me, like that somehow makes you better than the rest of us."

She forced herself to be brave. "You are currently trespassing, which is an arrestable offence."

"You going to arrest me, Mallory? I'd like to see you try."

She didn't have her handcuffs or pepper spray near to hand. It was all locked up in the boot of her car.

Was he actually going to hurt her?

He'd grabbed her, hadn't he? He'd shoved her. That was already assault. She was still sure she could talk her way out of this, though. She needed to listen, to empathise. She needed to remind him that she was a person, too. She tried to recall her training, how she was supposed to tell a hostage taker something personal about herself. But he already knew her, so that wasn't going to work.

She kept her voice calm. "What are you hoping to achieve here, Daniel? If you want to talk, that's fine, we can talk. I'll put the kettle on and make some tea, and we'll sit in the lounge. How does that sound?"

Her mobile phone sat in the inside pocket of her suit jacket, and its presence felt so huge to her it was like a brick. If she could get away from him for just a minute, she could put a call in that an officer was in need of help and her colleagues would be with her asap. They had each other's backs. If one of them was in distress, then they all hurt.

She still had a landline connected to the house as well. It had always felt safer than just relying on mobile phones, mainly because of Oliver, aware that if there was an emergency and one of them was able to get to the phone, then the call could be traced. The phone was in the entrance hall, only a matter of feet from where they stood now, but she knew there was little to no chance of her getting to the phone without Daniel snatching it away again. She would never have time to make a call, even if it only had three numbers.

But it seemed Daniel wasn't to be placated. "I don't want a fucking cup of tea from you."

"What is it you want then?" Mallory was starting to feel helpless, and she didn't like to feel that way.

How long until Ollie came home? Another hour or so? She didn't want him to walk into this, whatever *this* was. Frightening situations threw Oliver's progress off for months, and she couldn't stand for him to go backwards again, just because of this arsehole.

It didn't occur to her that *her* safety might actually be in jeopardy. Even now, she was still thinking about her brother.

"I want you to learn that you can't just go around treating people like playthings, like people you can just pick up and throw away again the moment you get bored of them."

Mallory almost laughed at that description of herself. She was so far from being that person, it was unbelievable. She never picked people up just to throw them away. She never picked people up, full stop. Every single interaction she ever had with anyone was thought out and balanced. It was only because Daniel was already in her home and already entwined in her life that she had even given him a second thought. As it had proven, that had been a massive mistake, and it wasn't one she planned on repeating.

But arguing with him wasn't going to help.

"I have learned that, Daniel," she said. "Please believe me. I have learned it. I won't be getting involved with anyone else anytime soon. Trust me."

He threw up his hands. "See, this is exactly what I was talking about. You're making out like this is all my fault—like I'm the one who did something wrong. So I paid a bit too much attention to your work life. Big fucking deal. I was interested in you. I wanted to get to know you, and somehow you've turned that into a crime." He laughed in disbelief. "Not everyone is out to get you, you know, Mallory. Some of us just want to be in your life."

The composure she'd been holding on to finally snapped. "You know what? My instincts to keep you at arm's length were right, and the fact we're having this conversation proves it. Do you think it's normal to shove somebody else into their house and basically stalk them when they tell you they're not interested anymore? This is hardly normal behaviour, is it?"

He shook his head at her. "See, you're twisting it around again, making out like you don't have any responsibility in what's happening now. If you'd only spoken nicely to me when I first asked, I wouldn't have to be here."

"Get out of my house, Daniel. I mean it. Leave. Now."

"Or what?" He took a step closer. "What are you going to do, Mallory?"

She was never going to get past him. His body blocked the way. She remembered the back door. It was locked, but if she managed to reach it, she might be able to get it open and run to a neighbour.

Hoping to catch him by surprise, she spun on her heels and ran. But she wasn't quick enough. She hadn't even made it to the end of the hallway before his fingers wrapped around her arm, hauling her back again.

His other fist caught her in the solar plexus, winding her. She folded in half, desperately trying to draw breath, tears welling. Her body went into shutdown, a screaming in her ears, only telling her that she couldn't get any oxygen into her lungs. He grabbed her by the back of her jacket and almost yanked her off her feet. Where was he taking her? She wanted to fight back, but she was still struggling to breathe, and now she almost tripped and fell.

He paused at the cupboard under the stairs, then used the hand not holding her to open it. It contained her hoover, a collection of old shoes, a couple of coats hanging from hooks. A few cardboard boxes resided right at the back, where the head height was the lowest, but she'd long forgotten what they contained.

It dawned on her that he intended to put her in there, and she pressed back against him. But she wasn't strong enough. He wasn't a big man, but she was smaller and lighter.

With a final shove, he sent her flying forwards, into the small space. Her feet caught on the bundles of loose shoes, and she went down, landing on her hands and knees, her face against the soft material of the winter coats.

To her intense relief, the band around her chest loosened, and she was able to suck in a long, blessed breath. Her lungs expanded and filled, and the panic and terror she'd experienced at not being able to breathe ebbed away.

Her relief didn't last long. Behind her, the understairs cupboard door banged shut, enclosing her in darkness.

There wasn't a lock on the door, but she heard the scrape of something being dragged across the floor and realised—too late—what was happening. She managed to twist around in the confined space, knocking things over with knees and elbows, and lunged for where she thought the handle would be. Her eyes hadn't yet got accustomed to the darkness, the only light being that from a tiny slit beneath the door. She floundered around for it for a few seconds, smacking her palms against the wood. Why couldn't she find it?

Then she realised there was no handle on this side of the door. Why would there be? It wasn't designed for people to come in and out of—just to get into. She had no way of opening it.

Tears pricked the backs of her eyes.

Oliver would be home soon. She couldn't have him coming home to discover her shut in the cupboard and with Daniel guarding it. What if Daniel tried to hurt Ollie to get back at her? He was trying to hurt her, and that would be the easiest way. She wanted to tell herself that he wouldn't do such a thing—that he had cared about Oliver, too—but right now she barely recognised the person he'd become. She couldn't believe she'd trusted him all that time with Oliver.

What did he want from her?

The way her mind worked made her want to see reason in his actions and come up with a solution, but sometimes things weren't as simple as that. People acted purely out of emotion, with no rational thought. Daniel probably didn't even know himself.

Embarrassment and anger seeped through her. How had she let this happen? She didn't want to call nine-nine-nine. To have sirens and flashing lights and all the neighbours peering out their window at her. It had been bad enough when they'd had the fire and everyone had been gossiping about her—and Oliver—making out as though it wasn't safe for Oliver to be left alone and that she was neglecting him. Now she'd have the same thing again, and this time it would be worse. She was a police officer, a detective, she should be able to handle arseholes like Daniel, but instead she'd ended up shut in under the stairs like a victim.

There was one thing Daniel hadn't taken into consideration, and that was the mobile phone still in the inside of her jacket pocket.

The minute he realised she had it, he would open the door to try and take it off her. If the phone rang, he would hear it. If it even buzzed with a notification, he might figure out where the noise came from.

She weighed up her chances. If he tried to take the phone off her, he would need to open the door. If he opened the door, she could try to get away. On the other hand, he might succeed, so she'd be left still trapped in the cupboard under the stairs and with no phone.

Moving carefully, she picked the phone out of her pocket. It was on twenty-eight percent battery, so at least she didn't need to worry about it dying just yet. If she brought the screen to life, would he see the change in light under the door? She tried to get a bearing on his position. She thought he'd dragged a chair from the kitchen and positioned it directly in front of the cupboard door, perhaps even wedging the back under the handle, just in case she found a way of getting it open. If he was sitting on it, his back would be to the door, in that case, so he hopefully wouldn't notice the change in light.

She braced herself, her breath caught, terrified her phone would buzz or ping with a notification, but it didn't. Did she dare switch off the sound? If she did, it would vibrate, and he might hear it. Even turning the volume up or down would create a beeping.

She pulled up Ryan's number. She hated that she was having to do this, but it felt like she had no choice. Either she asked for help, or Daniel would still be here when Oliver got home, and she couldn't handle the thought of Ollie having to deal with this on his own.

What if Ryan was busy and didn't check his phone? Or if his battery had run out and he'd forgotten to charge it? But she had worked with Ryan long enough to know that he always kept his phone close by in case of emergencies.

Tears of humiliation trickled down her cheeks. Ryan wouldn't put up with Daniel's bullshit, though. He'd know how to handle this. Sometimes men like Daniel only listened to other men.

Quickly, she typed out a text to her boss, her gut twisting and her heart heavy.

Help. Daniel has locked me in the cupboard under my stairs. I'm not hurt. Please don't phone back or text as he will hear it. Just come. No response team. Ollie not here.

Was she being selfish telling him not to bring a team? What if Daniel was armed and she was putting Ryan in danger? But she didn't want Oliver to come home to sirens and flashing lights. She wanted this to be dealt with as subtly as possible.

She stayed frozen, staring down at her phone, half wanting to get a message back from him to say he was on his way, while also hoping he didn't message back because then Daniel would hear it. Would it matter now if Daniel *did* hear the phone? She'd already messaged for help, and it wasn't as though Daniel could take that message back again. Oliver had his own mobile phone, and she contemplated sending him a message, too, but what would she say? Plus, he'd be far less likely to follow instructions or understand the importance of it. If she messaged him to tell him not to come home yet, he'd phone her and want to know why.

There was no point in banging on the door and screaming to be let out. She refused to give Daniel the satisfaction of hearing her upset. She remained sitting on the floor of her understairs cupboard, surrounded by old shoes and musty coats, and waited.

Chapter Twenty-Eight

D onna had just set a plate of chicken, chips, and salad down on the table in front of Ryan when his phone buzzed.

"Sorry," he told Donna. "It might be important."

She'd been a detective's wife for a long time. She understood that this wasn't really a job someone could clock in and out of, even if their rosters made it look that way.

He swiped the screen. A text from Mallory. He read it and frowned.

"Everything okay?" Donna asked.

"No, I don't think so. I just got a strange message from my sergeant. She says someone has locked her in a cupboard."

Donna's eyes widened. "What?"

He stood. "I'd better get over there."

"Is the person who locked her in still there? Don't you think you should call for backup?"

He probably should, but Mallory had asked him not to. He guessed she didn't want this on the record.

"I think it's something I can handle. I know who she says did it."

Donna reached out and touched his arm. "Ryan, that's really not sensible."

"If I think there's anything to worry about, I'll call for backup right away, I promise."

He leaned down and kissed her on the mouth. "I'll be back."

"Be careful."

He hurried from the house. Mallory's home was about fifteen minutes away, but right now, those fifteen minutes felt like hours. He should phone this in and see if there was a response vehicle closer, but he also wanted to respect her wishes.

Anger and indignation on Mallory's behalf rose inside him. That someone would dare to do that to his serious, smart sergeant made him want to tear that particular person's head off. He needed to keep his cool. He didn't want to rush into things and make it worse for Mallory.

He wasn't going to let this arsehole get away with it, though. She might not want a response car, but he fully intended on arresting the prick for assault and false imprisonment of a police officer. He'd make sure Mallory got a restraining order on Daniel, too. He wished she'd told him she was having problems with the bloke. He remembered that they'd been out for a few drinks a couple of times. She'd said it wasn't working out, but Ryan assumed Daniel hadn't taken no for an answer.

Why had she felt she couldn't tell him? He'd been aware things weren't quite right with her, and had even asked her directly, but she'd insisted everything had been fine. How long had this guy been hassling her for?

He put the flashing lights on in the dashboard and drove as fast as he dared. It wasn't late yet, and there was still plenty of traffic on the roads, forcing him to use his horn and roll down his window, using arm gestures—polite ones—to get other drivers to pull out of his way.

"Come on, you idiots," he muttered.

Was Daniel hurting Mallory? If she was locked in somewhere, he hoped that meant Daniel didn't have access to her, but there was nothing stopping him from opening the door again.

He pictured his sergeant beaten and bloodied, or worse, and his heart clenched. She'd said she was unharmed in her message, but that didn't mean she'd stay that way. What if Daniel had killed her by the time Ryan got there? How would their team function without her? How would her brother manage? He couldn't imagine Oliver trying to live through that kind of pain and without his sister's support.

He reached Mallory's place and swung the car into an empty spot, not caring how badly he was parked. He climbed out and hurried around to the boot, grabbing handcuffs, pepper spray, and an extendable baton.

He didn't have a key, so instead, he hammered on the front door. "Open the door, Daniel. It's the police. I know you're in there."

There was movement on the other side of the textured pane of glass.

Ryan used the end of his baton to smash the glass pane, offering a silent apology to Mallory for the damage, and reached through the gap and unlocked the door from the inside.

Farther down the hallway, a young man stood beside a chair, the back of which had been wedged beneath the handle of the cupboard under the stairs. Ryan knew his sergeant was in there.

"Step away from the door," he instructed the other man.

Daniel faced him. "Why the fuck should I do anything you say?"

"Because I'm the police, and I've got backup on the way, and you have assaulted one of our own. If you think you're going anywhere from here other than jail, you are very much mistaken."

Ryan wanted to free Mallory, but he also wanted to get Daniel into a set of cuffs. Ryan was blocking the front door, but could Daniel get out the back? He tried to predict the other man's next move, figuring out if he was more likely to run than fight. Ryan scanned Daniel's body and hands, checking for any weapons he might have held or hidden about his person, but there was nothing obvious.

Should he tell him to let Mallory out of the cupboard before arresting him?

But no, if he released Mallory, there was the chance he'd grab her and use her as a human shield to protect himself.

"Are you okay, Mallory?" Ryan called out.

"Ryan?" Her voice came muffled from under the stairs.

"Are you hurt?"

"No, I'm okay."

Now he'd ascertained she was okay and not in need of any immediate medical help, he could focus his attention on arresting her ex—if he even had the right to call himself that.

Ryan wasn't going to allow himself to be intimidated by this idiot. He had about four inches and close to twenty years on him.

"Daniel, I am arresting you for the assault and false imprisonment of a police officer. You do not have to say anything. But, it may harm your defence if you do not mention when questioned something which you later rely on in court. Anything you do say may be given in evidence."

"Fuck you," Daniel replied, taking a step backwards and yanking the chair out from under the handle, positioning it between the two of them instead.

"Don't be stupid." Ryan remained calm. "All you're going to do is make things worse for yourself."

Daniel picked up the chair and threw it at Ryan, then turned and ran for the back of the house. Ryan easily deflected the piece of furniture, and it crashed to the floor. Ryan took after him. As he passed the stair cupboard door, he pulled it open, freeing Mallory.

Daniel had reached the back door, trying to yank it open. When he realised it was locked, he spun around to face Ryan again.

"I don't want to have to get physical with you, but I will," Ryan warned him. "There's nowhere for you to go now."

He became aware of Mallory behind him. "You okay?"

He risked a glance backwards. Mallory's face was even paler than normal, but her jaw was set in a line of determination. Her nostrils flared with anger, and there was a sharp glint to her eyes.

"I'm fine. I just want to see this arsehole in cuffs."

"I'm working on it."

Daniel darted for the window, clambering up onto the kitchen worktop, throwing things off as he went. A mug hit the floor and smashed, shortly followed by a salt shaker, and then a glass container filled with pasta. Thankfully, that didn't break and instead just rolled to one side. He was still making a hell of a mess, though.

Ryan moved forwards and grabbed one of his feet, dodging a kick, and yanked him off. Daniel fell, hard, winding himself on the floor. Ryan straddled Daniel, pinning him to the floor and yanked his hands behind his back.

Rage descended over him, threatening to wipe out all sensible thought. His protectiveness for Mallory only served to intensify his anger.

He'd felt this way one time before, hadn't he? When he'd finally confronted the young man who'd mowed down Hayley with his car and then driven off and hidden for long enough so that whatever alcohol had been in his system could no longer be recorded. Flashes of the night burst into his head like screenshots of a film—a car boot slamming shut, the river rushing below, a rope tied around a leg. Ryan shook his head slightly, trying to dispel them. Intrusive thoughts, that's all they were, trying to put false memories into his head. They were always worse during moments of stress. They weren't the truth.

But the urge to take out his anger on the man now trapped beneath him refused to let go. How dare Daniel think he had any right to treat Mallory like that. How dare any man think he had the power to control a woman, just because he might be physically bigger and stronger. Mallory was a hundred times the person Daniel would ever be. This scumbag deserved to go down for a very long time, but the truth was that he probably wouldn't even serve time. The best they could probably hope for was a suspended sentence and an order to stay away from Mallory, and half the time a restraining order wasn't worth the paper it was written on. How many times had men been served restraining orders and gone on to kill their partners anyway?

"Ryan?"

Mallory's voice filtered through to him.

"Ryan? It's okay."

He was still shoving Daniel hard against the floor.

"Get the fuck off me!" Daniel protested. "That hurts!"

Ryan forced himself to come back to the present, to remind himself who he was and of his duty to the law. Hurting this man wasn't going to help Mallory.

He cautioned him again, making sure Daniel wouldn't be able to use a technicality as an excuse to get off—and cuffed his wrists.

"Don't think for one second that you're just going to get a slap on the wrist for this," he told Daniel. "The law doesn't look too kindly on people who abuse one of their own."

Daniel tried to yank away from Ryan but wasn't going anywhere. "It wasn't abuse! Get the fuck off me. Talk about exaggerating things!"

Ryan narrowed his eyes. "No? What would you call it then?"

"Teaching that bitch a lesson."

It took all of Ryan's self-control not to bash Daniel's head against the cupboards.

He hauled Daniel to his feet and marched him out of the house and towards the car. Mallory followed close behind, her arms wrapped around her torso in a combination of comfort and protection.

Ryan put him in the back of the car and got on the phone to call for backup.

When Daniel was finally shut away, Mallory seemed to slump inwards, as though she'd finally allowed herself to give in.

"Thank you," she said, "I didn't know who else to call."

He rubbed the side of her arm to offer some comfort. "Are you okay?"

Her face was pinched, and she blinked hard, clearly trying not to cry.

"Hey, it's okay," he said, "you're safe now."

She straightened and nodded but still didn't look at him directly. "Thank you for coming."

"Are you hurt? Do I need to call an ambulance?"

"I'm fine. He winded me, that was all. I don't need to see a doctor."

"He assaulted you. You understand this needs to go on record?"

"I do. I won't let him get away with it. I won't let him go on and do this to someone else."

"He doesn't have any record of this kind of behaviour?"

"No. It would have been picked up by the charity otherwise. They always run background checks because the people they work with are vulnerable. It would have been noted if he had a history of violence or stalking. Why he decided to start with me, I guess I'll never know."

"Don't torture yourself trying to figure out why he fixated on you. Sometimes there's no rational answer to these things and you will only drive yourself crazy trying to figure it out."

She sniffed. "I know. It's going to be hard not to overanalyse everything, though, trying to work out if I did or said anything to give him the wrong idea. I don't know...maybe I did."

"It doesn't matter what you said or did. Once you'd told him you weren't interested anymore, he should have listened. You're allowed to change your mind about someone, and, in this case, you were clearly right to."

"Thanks, boss."

"Do you need to take some time off? I can arrange for you to speak to someone about what you've just gone through. It'll be a trauma for you, Mallory. You need to process it."

She sighed. "Thanks, but the last thing I want is to take time off. It's better if I stay busy. I don't want to sit around, thinking and worrying, when I could be doing something productive. We still don't know who killed Tai, and I'd hate to sit around doing nothing, knowing that her killer is still out there, laughing at us."

He understood. He preferred to stay busy, too. Sitting around with too much time on his hands was the worst thing he could do for his mental health. If he didn't occupy his thoughts with something—normally work—memories he'd rather forget would creep in. His worst thoughts would be about the moments before Hayley had been killed, going over every tiny little moment, wondering if he'd only done something slightly different, she wouldn't have been in the path of the drunk driver. If only he hadn't let that driver out at the intersection on his way to the school. If only he hadn't stopped to say hello to Hayley's teacher. If only...if only...if only... He beat himself up over the things he'd said to her during the days before her death, wondering if he'd been loving enough, kind enough, if she'd known exactly how important she was to him.

"I'm glad you were able to phone me. I wish you'd told me sooner that you were having issues with that arsehole."

She pressed her lips together. "I kept hoping he would just give up and go away, but he didn't."

"We'll make sure he does now, okay?"

The flashing lights of approaching response vehicles cut through the darkened sky.

Mallory winced. "Something else for the neighbours to gossip about."

"They giving you trouble, too?"

"Oh, you know what people can be like. Ever since the fire, they've all liked to poke their nose in. They say it's in the interest of safety, claiming that the fire was proof Ollie shouldn't be left alone, even though it literally could have happened to anyone, and now they'll see the police here and decide it's another reason to think I'm an irresponsible, bad neighbour."

He grimaced. "Sorry, I didn't have any choice."

"I understand. It's not your fault."

"Have you thought about moving?" he suggested.

She let out a long sigh. "This is our family home. Our parents moved out of it to allow Ollie and me to live here. I couldn't imagine how moving from the only place he's ever known would affect him."

"What about how things affect you?" he asked in concern.

"I'm fine," she said, then repeated it, as though she was trying to convince herself. "I'm fine."

"You sure you're going to be all right for work in the morning?"

"Absolutely." She wrapped her arms around her body. "I'll give my statement then, if that's okay?"

"Of course."

"Thanks, because Ollie's going to be—" She broke off. "Oh, shit. He's home already. What am I going to tell him?"

"That you had some police friends around and had a bit of a party that got out of hand, but everyone's going now."

She exhaled. "Thanks, boss."

"No problem. I'll see you in the morning."

Chapter Twenty-Nine

The following morning, Mallory brought him a large coffee from a takeaway restaurant and placed it on his desk.

"Thanks again for last night. I've just given my statement, and Daniel is still in custody. I hope I didn't interrupt anything important?"

Ryan assessed her, checking for any signs that she was still shaken up from the night before and shouldn't be working. She seemed just like normal, though, maybe a little tired, but that was all.

"No, it was fine," he said. "I was just having dinner."

"With Donna?"

"Yeah, with Donna."

"I'm sorry I disturbed it."

"Don't be silly, Donna understands. She's been the wife of a police officer for a long time—I mean, she *had* been."

Mallory raised her eyebrows. "The two of you are back together then?"

"I'm not sure. We're not putting any labels on it. Less pressure that way."

She smiled. "I'm pleased for you, Ryan. You deserve a little happiness."

"So do you," he said.

She gave a cold chuckle. "I tried that, remember. Look where it got me."

"Don't let one bad egg put you off."

"The trouble is that sometimes it feels like there's more bad eggs than good. If you were given a box of six eggs and told half of them were rotten, but you had to eat the bad ones to get to the good, you probably wouldn't want to eat any of them either."

He lifted his coffee cup and tapped it to hers. "Touché."

She hesitated. "Oliver won't be called as a witness, will he? I mean, he saw some of what Daniel was like, but I really don't want to put him through that."

"I'm sure we won't need to get your brother involved. I assume you kept the messages you received from Daniel and a record of the times he stalked you?"

She shivered slightly at the word 'stalked' but nodded. "Yes, of course."

"And obviously you have me as a witness as well. We have enough to charge him and to get a restraining order so he stays well away from both you and Ollie."

From across the office, Shonda Dawson hurried towards them.

"Boss," she said, "the search team at the Avon gorge have just found Tai's phone. It was wedged into a small crevasse in the rock. It must have fallen from her hand or pocket when she was thrown."

He resisted the urge to punch the air. Finally, something had gone their way.

"What sort of condition is it in?"

She handed him over a printed photograph of an iPhone 13. The screen was completely smashed.

Ryan huffed out a breath. "I guess it would have been too much luck for it to have been intact."

"Yes, but it shouldn't cause a problem for digital forensics as long as the internal storage isn't damaged."

"Let's hope not. Get it over to Isaac, asap."

He needed to speak to Isaac himself, see if his team had managed to get into the phones and laptops taken from the Jennings' property yet. Isaac was also checking the profiles of any men who might have made contact with Chloe Jennings.

His phone rang, distracting him for a moment.

He answered, "DI Chase."

"Hi, this is Tanya from Florals and Blooms."

It took him a minute to figure out why a florist was calling him, and then he remembered the flowers he'd had sent over to the hospital where Craig's mother had been taken.

"Oh, yes. Is everything okay? Did the payment not go through or something?"

He was distracted, aware he had more important things to be dealing with than a flower delivery.

"No, nothing like that. The thing is..."

She trailed off, and his irritation grew.

"What is it?" he said.

"There is no Mrs Penn on the stroke ward or even in the hospital. We asked all over. No one had heard of her. Are you sure you got the right place? Or even the right name?"

He checked the note he'd scribbled with the name and hospital on and read it back to her.

"Yes, that's definitely what we have as well," she confirmed.

"Strange. Okay, don't worry. Thank you for trying."

She still didn't end the call. "Umm, I'm sorry, but we won't be able to give a refund. We made up the bouquet and tried to deliver. We held up our end of the transaction."

"That's fine. I won't be requesting a refund. Are you still at the hospital?"

"Yes, just outside the main entrance."

"Give them to someone who needs cheering up. Someone who'll appreciate them."

She sounded brighter. "Okay, Will do, DI Chase."

He ended the call.

That was strange. Perhaps Craig's mother had a different surname. He took out his phone and called Craig's mobile number. It rang until the answerphone picked up. He considered leaving a message but then didn't bother. The flowers were such a trivial thing, he didn't want to bother Craig with it or create a situation where he'd need to reorder them.

Ryan had enough on his plate with the case.

Chapter Thirty

Faye found a small hotel that didn't cost an arm and a leg and promised Chloe they'd be able to stay there for a few days. The television in the room had more than five channels, so at least it helped to keep Chloe entertained, and it was just off the town's high street, too.

She'd given in to Chloe's cries of boredom, so now the two of them browsed the small high street, popping into shops and trying on clothes to keep themselves entertained.

Chloe smiled and laughed as she tried on items she hated—just for the fun of it. Faye watched her daughter, feeling like she was living in some kind of warped reality, like she was on the outside of a window, staring in. How could Chloe act so normally while Faye was in a daze? She didn't think she'd ever smile properly again.

They exited the shop, and Chloe drew to a halt and grabbed Faye's arm. Faye's heart lurched, certain they'd been found.

"Mum, look! There's a Starbucks over the road. Can we get coffee?"

Faye's whole body slumped in relief.

"No, Chloe. I can't afford that. We need to make our money last."

"Seriously?" Chloe raised her eyebrows. "It's just coffee. I'm not asking you to buy me a bloody car or something."

"And I said no. We can buy a whole jar of coffee for the price we'd pay for a single frappa-bloody-wotsit."

Chloe rolled her eyes. "It's called a Frappuccino, Mum. Jeez."

"I don't care what it's called. I said no."

"I'm almost eighteen years old. Why am I still having to beg my mother to buy me things?"

Exasperation rose inside her. "You know why!"

Chloe threw up her hands. "You went and got money out before we left. I could have done the same."

Faye turned to face her daughter. "And whose money would you be spending then, Chloe? Huh? Tell me that. Just the thought of how you'd have 'earned' that money makes me sick to my stomach."

"You're completely overreacting, as usual."

"Overreacting? A girl is dead! You think that's overreacting?"

Chloe fell silent and pressed her lips together. When she spoke again, it was in a more subdued tone. "I'm just saying that how I earned the money isn't as big a deal as you're making it. It was just exchanging a few suggestive messages and some photos. Everyone does it these days."

"Not for money, they don't, and not for older men who are preying on teenage girls. The whole thing makes me sick. Do you really believe they wouldn't want to meet you eventually? That they wouldn't expect a date out of this? And by date, I'm not talking about a nice meal in a posh restaurant."

Chloe pouted. "They might have wanted that, but it didn't mean they were going to get it."

"You didn't think that might piss the wrong people off? And don't even get me started on how beginning your adult life being co-dependent on an older man is wrong on so many levels. I thought I'd raised you better than this."

"Don't judge me," Chloe cried. "I'm the one taking advantage of them. It's not my fault if men want to pay for stuff for younger women."

"But you're not a woman, are you? You're still a girl. You're not even eighteen yet, and even when you do turn eighteen, you'll still be a child in my mind. You haven't done any of the things that makes a person a woman. You don't even pay your own bills, for pity's sake. The reason these men like so much younger women isn't just because of your appearance. It's also because they don't want a woman their own age who can see through their bullshit and tell them where to go." Faye was shaking now, and she forced herself to take a breath and calm herself down. She sensed people on the streets staring at them and lowered her voice. "Look, Chloe, this isn't just about me being a prude. A girl is dead. That's the sort of thing that happens when you get involved in websites like that."

Chloe stared at her. "We should go to the police then."

"We can't. You know we can't. They protect their own."

"We can't keep moving forever. Maybe we can place an anonymous phone call or email or something to the investigating team? Tell them everything."

Faye shook her head. "They'd be able to trace the call, and what if *he's* the one who picks up the message? He could just delete it and use it to find us. Then you'd end up the same as Tai."

The terror in her daughter's face was like ice to her heart. She pulled Chloe in for a hug, her fingers in her soft hair. Her daughter trembled in her arms. Faye wanted to cry as well. She wanted to break down and scream until her throat was raw and tear the whole world to pieces. But she was a mother, even though her child was practically grown—and certainly old enough to do things she shouldn't have been—and her instinct was to protect them both.

"The police still might figure it out on their own," she said. "There will be clues, even if they haven't found them yet. If that happens, no one needs to know you were involved. We'll just go home and tell everyone that we needed a break. There's no reason people won't believe us. People go on holidays all the time."

"Okay, Mum."

"Let's go back to the hotel, take a nap. I'm exhausted."

Chloe's shoulders slumped beneath her touch, and she gave the Starbucks one final, longing glance. "Sure, Mum. Whatever you want."

Chapter Thirty-One

Ryan's phone rang. "DI Chase."

"Ryan, it's Isaac Madakor."

"Isaac. How are you? Did you manage to get anything off the phones?"

He hesitated. "Can we talk in private. You're going to want to see this. Or maybe not want to, but you need to."

"Umm, sure. Same place?"

"I'll be there in five."

Ryan let his team know he was just popping out for half an hour and then left the building to head to the café. Isaac was already there, at the same table, his laptop already open. He didn't get to his feet as Ryan entered, and his expression was serious.

Something twisted Ryan's guts. What was this about? It didn't seem like anything good.

"What have you got for me, Isaac," he said, slipping into the seat.

"A couple of things, but they're both linked. I've been going through the profiles of the men who've been messaging Chloe Jennings, seeing if I can connect the usernames to any email addresses or Google accounts, and then, if I've found something under one of them, crosschecking the names with our records. Anyway, one in particular caught my attention."

"Who is it?"

"He was under the username *ArcanePenMan*. I was able to track the username back to a LinkedIn profile."

Ryan raised his eyebrows. "Wow, that was stupid of them. Guess we can always rely on the stupidity of criminals."

Isaac didn't smile. "There's a name and photograph." He typed something into his laptop and then turned the screen so Ryan could see.

Ryan recognised the picture instantly.

"No." His head spun, and he gripped the edges of the table. He didn't want to believe it, but what choice did he have when it was right there in front of him.

DC Craig Penn.

"Holy shit." He covered his mouth with his hand. "Penn came up with some story about his mother being sick, but that must have been a lie. I tried to send some flowers to the hospital, and the delivery person said there was no one by that name there. Craig must have felt like we were getting too close and so he took off."

"That's not all," Isaac said. "I was also able to get into Tai's phone and check the photographs on it."

He showed Ryan another image.

This was of Craig with his arm around the murdered girl. He wasn't looking directly into the camera, so it seemed as though Tai had picked up her phone and taken a pic while he was unaware. No wonder. He never would have wanted a photograph of himself on her phone.

"Can you tell when that photograph was taken?" Ryan asked.

"Yes, it's time stamped. It was taken on the second of June."

"Almost three weeks ago now."

Did that mean Craig was responsible for Tai's death? He didn't want to believe it of one of his own. But then why would he lie? Craig had run because he didn't want to be around when they uncovered the truth about his involvement in the case.

Something else occurred to Ryan. Had Craig left to track down Chloe? Did he know where she was?

Craig had always been a bit of a live wire, but Ryan put it down to his age. He liked to go out drinking, could be a bit loud and overconfident. But a killer? To push a seventeen-year-old girl off a bridge like that? And Craig was a police officer. He'd have known there were cameras. But had he realised they were infrared cameras? Maybe he'd thought the dark and fog would have been enough to cover his actions, and then when he'd learnt they weren't, had run?

Ryan thought of something else. They still didn't know where Chloe Jennings or her mother were. Was Craig the person they were running from?

Ryan wanted to lash out, to kick at something and shove the laptop off the table, but he was an adult not a moody teenager, so he held himself in check.

"Thank you for this information, Isaac. Can you keep it to yourself? I'm going to need to talk to my boss about how we're going to handle this."

This was going to be a disaster as far as public relations went for the force. There had been a number of incidents over the past couple of years that hadn't made them look good, and now they were going to have another one. A police officer killing a seventeen-year-old girl was as bad as it got.

Then he checked himself. They didn't know for sure that Craig Penn was responsible for killing Tai. Yes, he had a connection with both the girls and had been acting inappropriately by using the dark web to use websites to secure dates with girls who weren't yet eighteen, but had any of those things broken the law?

Now that Craig was uncontactable didn't go in his favour. To any outside person, it screamed of guilt.

TEN MINUTES LATER, Ryan was sitting in DCI Hirst's office, showing her the evidence Isaac had found.

"We need to find Craig Penn," he said.

Mandy nodded. "I agree. We need his name and photograph circulated, and check to see if he's left the country. He'd have had time to do that by now. We need to keep this from the press for as long as possible. If there is any chance he's innocent, I don't want the reporters getting hold of a story when there isn't one."

"He's tried to run," Ryan pointed out. "That doesn't speak of the actions of an innocent man."

Her lips thinned. "I agree, it doesn't."

"He lied to me. Lied directly to my face. He told me his mother was deathly sick in hospital, but what he was really doing was running away."

"Lying to get time off is a disciplinary issue, though," she pointed out, "it doesn't bring a prison sentence with it."

"What about paying a teenage girl for explicit photographs and possibly even more? Even if he didn't kill her, that's still not going to reflect well on the force."

"No, but I'd like to imagine it's something we can deal with internally. Obviously he won't be working for us anymore.

We've lost our trust in him. He will be suspended with immediate effect while our enquiries are being carried out."

Ryan nodded. "Of course. I'm with you. I just hate the thought of the media getting hold of this story and blowing it up before we've even had the chance to question the people involved." He sighed and ran his hand over his face. "I just wish Craig had come to me and told me the truth before running. Yes, his job would still be on the line, but at least we could have got ahead of things."

"That he didn't only makes him appear even guiltier. I know we hate to think one of our own is capable of doing something so horrific, but we can't allow ourselves to be blindsided by the fact that he is a police officer. If anything, we need to hold him to a higher regard than we would a civilian."

"Agreed. I need to see the footage from the CCTV on the bridge again, try and figure out if there's a chance the person on it is Craig."

Now he had an idea who it might have been, he needed to study it. He felt sure he'd know if the person was Craig—someone he'd spent time with almost every day for the past few years.

A knock came at the door, and Linda's head popped through. "Sorry to interrupt, but we've found Faye Jennings. She's used her credit card at a Starbucks just outside of Perth in Scotland. I've got local officers heading to the area now. It's unlikely she'll still be there, but they've been instructed to look out for the car she exchanged hers for as well."

"That's excellent news, Linda. Thanks. I'll be right there." He turned back to his boss. "Assuming Chloe is with her mother, we might be able to hear their side of things very soon."

He left the office and paused outside the door. Conversations like that were never comfortable. He couldn't help feeling responsible. Craig had been on his team, and Ryan had never noticed anything was up with him. How could he have? The messages were all done on a private computer, and what Craig did outside of his work time normally wouldn't have been any concern of Ryan's. Now, he felt like he'd let everyone down.

Still, he kept turning the possibility of Craig murdering Tai over in his mind, trying to picture the event as though he was standing right beside them when it had happened. He tried to picture Craig's face on the black-and-white, fuzzy image of the person who'd pushed Tai over the bridge. He tried to imagine the conversation that had happened between the two of them moments before she'd fallen. Tai had been waiting for someone that night. Had that someone been Craig?

Ryan approached Linda for more information on the bank records.

"As we expected," she said, "up until now, Faye hadn't used the card since the morning after Tai Moore died, when she went to a cashpoint and withdrew what money she could on her cards."

"Sounds as though she didn't want to use her card while she was away."

"Exactly. Why would she do that, if not because she didn't want to be found?"

"We have to ask ourselves exactly why she didn't want to be found? Is she protecting her daughter? Maybe whoever killed Tai could have it in for Chloe as well."

He hadn't yet informed the rest of his team about Craig's involvement, but the moment he made the suggestion, it was Craig's face that sprang into his mind. Were the Jenningses running from Craig? Had he gone after them?

"The girls didn't use their real names," Linda said. "How did he, or she, find out who they are in real life?"

"Bristol isn't exactly a big city. Maybe he just recognised them. Or if this person convinced the girls that they'd be better working outside of the website, they might have been silly enough to give their real names."

"And bank accounts," she commented.

He grimaced. "Exactly."

"You think whoever killed Tai might have gone after Chloe?"

"If she knows something, it's possible."

"Why not come to us? Why run? They could just hand over the name of the person who did this, and we'd put them behind bars. Surely that's better than abandoning your entire life and going on the run?"

It occurred to Ryan that if Isaac hadn't found out that information about Craig, and they'd still managed to track down Faye and Chloe, they'd have been delivering the mother and daughter straight into Craig's hands.

He was going to have to fill his team in on these most recent developments. Though it sickened him to have to do so, they weren't going to be able to do their jobs properly without all the information.

"Linda, can you gather everyone to the incident room. There's something I need to tell you all."

Chapter Thirty-Two

Bang-bang-bang!

Faye bolted upright on the bed, her heart racing. Someone was hammering at the door. She glanced over at Chloe, who was sitting on her own bed on the other side of the room. Chloe caught her looking and quickly hid something behind her back.

"Faye Jennings? Chloe Jennings? This is the police. Please open up."

Faye's breath caught. The police? No. How did they find them?

Tears pricked her eyes, and her whole body trembled.

Bang-bang-bang!

"We know you're in there. Open the door."

She didn't have any choice. They'd break the door down if they had to. Slowly, she got off the bed.

"Mum?" Chloe whispered.

"I have to open it."

She went to the door. With a shaking hand, she opened it to reveal two uniformed police officers standing on the other side.

"Faye Jennings?" the police officer asked.

She nodded.

"I'm DC Brian Coomber. I'm afraid you're going to need to come with us. You're wanted for questioning in regard to the murder of Tai Moore." He glanced over at Chloe. "Chloe Jennings?"

Chloe nodded, too.

"You're going to need to come with us, as well," he said.

Chloe remained huddled on the bed.

He stepped closer. "Sorry, Miss. But you have to come with us now."

He took hold of Chloe's arm to hold her up, and as he pulled her forward, Chloe had no choice but to let go of the thing she'd been hiding.

A Starbucks cup fell to the floor, spilling the milky-brown liquid all over the carpet.

Faye stared at it, her mouth open. Then what had happened and how the police had found them sank in. Chloe must have waited until Faye had fallen asleep and then took her card and went out and bought herself the bloody coffee. With the tap options to pay for things on cards these days, she hadn't even needed to know the PIN.

"You stupid bitch!" she cried. "You stupid, selfish little bitch!"

She launched at her daughter, her hands raised to slap her senseless. Only the police officer grabbing her and yanking her back again prevented her from unleashing her anger and fear on her teenager.

Chloe cowered, terrified, her eyes wide. "I'm sorry, Mum. I only wanted a coffee. I didn't think it would hurt."

Faye burst into tears. "Why couldn't you have just listened to me? Why couldn't you have done what you're told for one goddamned time in your life? It's over now, Chloe. Do you understand that? Everything we've ever known is over."

Chapter Thirty-Three

"Ryan, I thought you'd want to know that Craig's been picked up in Plymouth."

Ryan put down his pen and looked up at his DCI. He guessed this was good news, though it didn't feel that way.

"Plymouth? What was he doing there?"

"Getting a ferry to Spain we think."

Ryan let out a breath. "Jesus, Craig. What was he thinking? The DC couldn't appear guiltier if he tried.

"He's been taken to Plymouth police station and he'll be interviewed there," she said. "Obviously, we couldn't have members of our team interviewing him, not with everyone knowing him so personally."

"That was the right thing to do."

Linda also joined them. "I've just got word that Chloe and Faye Jennings have been picked up by the Scottish police. They're both being transported down to Bristol now, but obviously it'll take some time for them to get here. They're both pretty shaken up, which is understandable."

Realisation dawned on Ryan. "They didn't come to us for help because they knew Craig was a police officer?"

"Certainly seems that way."

DCI Hirst huffed out a breath and shook her head. "I hate that. I always want members of the public to feel we're the people to turn to, no matter what. We should always be the good guys in their eyes. That's why we need to come down hard on Craig, even if he is innocent of killing that girl. The rest of the force need to understand that we expect impeccable reputations with our officers. This isn't the place to tolerate sleazy behaviour like that."

"When are they interviewing Craig?" he asked her.

"Soon, I believe."

"I'd like to watch remotely."

She nodded. "I'm sure that can be arranged."

"Thanks. I'll let you know when I've heard from Plymouth, and I'll keep you informed how the interviews go with Chloe and her mother, too."

Ryan didn't think anyone here was going to be getting any sleep tonight.

RYAN SAT IN THE ROOM with the monitor and a set of headphones clamped to his ears.

He was looking at an interview room over a hundred miles away, with what would soon be his ex-colleague sitting on one side of the table and two detectives Ryan didn't know on the other. Next to Craig was a woman in a suit—a solicitor, he assumed.

The questioning had already started, running through the groundwork around Craig's name, address, and, of course, his job.

Ryan always struggled when other people were doing the interviews and he was just stuck in this room, watching. He wanted to get in there and ask his own questions, but he knew the other detectives were more than capable.

Something twisted in his gut at the thought of his colleagues. How had he got things so wrong about Craig? He normally trusted his instincts. Did he really have a murderer working with him?

"DC Craig Penn," the detective said, "where were you the night Tai Moore was killed?"

"Home, alone."

"Can anyone verify that?"

"No. Like I said, I was alone." Craig sat back. "I know how this looks, but I didn't kill that girl, I swear it."

The male detective appeared to be leading the interview. "You don't deny that you were using a website called *www-dot-SearchingBenefits-dot-com* and that your username is *ArcanePenMan?*"

Craig shook his head. "No, I don't, but using a dating website doesn't make me a killer. I'm single. I didn't think I was doing any harm."

"You must have known there was some harm involved. You were on the dark web. You knew you'd come across things that were illegal. It's the whole point of using it. You wanted to cover your tracks."

Craig threaded his fingers together. "I was curious, that's all. I'd seen this site mentioned online, and so I scoped it out. Then Tai and I got chatting via the messaging option. She said she was local."

"You sent her money for pictures of herself. She was seventeen, for God's sake."

"Yes, but not underage. It's not illegal."

"How about morally underage? As police officers, we should hold ourselves to the highest of standards. How can we possibly expect people to uphold the law when we're traversing the edges of breaking it ourselves?"

In the room in Bristol, Ryan pushed away thoughts of Cole Fielding and the mysterious circumstances surrounding his death.

Craig rubbed his hand across his face. "I didn't mean it to get so out of hand. I...I got carried away. I told myself that we had a connection, that she was mature for her age.

"Jesus Christ, Craig," Ryan muttered, though Craig couldn't hear him.

Craig continued, "Then she found out that I'd dropped into her friend's DMs on the site, and she lost it. She was furious. She thought we had something special, and I tried to tell her that it was just an arrangement, that she was on the site for other men to send messages to, so I should be able to send other girls messages as well. But she was insanely jealous. She said she was going to expose me. She'd figured out what I did for a living. Then she asked for more money. She was basically blackmailing me."

"Wasn't that the arrangement anyway?" the detective said. "That you gave her money for her time and company?"

"Yes, but it was different now. I didn't want her time or company when she was acting like that." He dropped his head. "I might have said some stuff, too. Things like that if she tried to bring me down, then I'd expose her. I said she was no better than a whore and I'd make sure everyone she knew found out about it."

"What about Chloe Jennings?"

Craig rubbed his hand across his face. "I didn't know the two of them were friends, but then I found out Tai had told her all about me, about what my job was. When I found out that she'd taken off after Tai had been killed, I thought she was going to drop me in it. I thought I might be able to get in touch with her, but I couldn't. I only wanted to talk to her, I swear. I wanted to know what she was thinking."

"You wanted to shut her up?"

He sat up straight. "I—no, not like that! I didn't want her to tell anyone about me, of course I didn't. But I didn't want to shut her up like that. I was never a danger to her."

The detective frowned. "Would Tai have said the same?"

"Yes, because I didn't hurt that girl. I definitely didn't throw her off the bridge. Surely you can see that from the CCTV footage."

"You've seen that footage, Craig. You know it's impossible to tell who it is."

"There's no proof I killed her. I'm a detective. I know you need actual evidence, not just circumstantial. I might have known her—I even sent her money—but that's all. I didn't kill her."

"We have motive and opportunity, and then there's your actions afterwards. You went after another girl. What the fuck were you thinking, Craig? Why didn't you just tell the truth?"

"Because I knew how bad it looked. I knew I'd end up in this position now."

Craig put his head in his hands.

He truly did seem defeated.

Ryan stared at the image. Was Craig really a killer?

Chapter Thirty-Four

Twelve hours after they'd first been located, both Chloe and Faye Jennings arrived back in Bristol to be interviewed.

Because of the seriousness of the case, the two were separated and a responsible adult brought in to sit in on the interview with Chloe.

Mallory took the lead on the interview with the girl.

"Chloe, do you know why you're here?"

Chloe nodded. "Because of what happened to Tai."

"What *did* happen to Tai?"

"Someone pushed her off the bridge."

"Do you know who that person was?"

"I-I'm not sure."

"We believe you may have been one of the last people to see Tai alive." She pushed a printout of the CCTV footage from the McDonald's restaurant onto the table between them. "This is you and Tai on the evening before Tai was killed, is that right?"

Chloe peered down at the image. "Yes, that's right. We'd arranged to meet up earlier that day to talk about stuff."

"Stuff? Can you elaborate on that?"

Her tongue snuck out and swiped across her lower lip. "The sugar babies site we were both on."

"What was there to talk about?"

"Tai wanted me to close down my account."

"Why?"

Chloe shrugged. "Because she was jealous."

"Of what?"

"Of the men I was attracting on there."

Mallory would come back to that. She wanted to get into the details of what Tai's final hours had been like first.

"In the security footage from McDonald's, two young men approach you. They spend about a minute talking to you both. Did you know them?"

"No. They came over and asked how old we were and then asked for our snaps."

"Your snaps?"

"Yeah, our Snapchats. We told them we were fifteen, just to get rid of them. They acted all butt-hurt because of how old we'd said we were and then they said we were fit anyway." She rolled her eyes. "They were idiots."

"Did you see them again after you left?"

"No."

"You don't think they might have followed Tai or hurt her?"

"I don't know, but I don't think so. We have stuff like that happen to us all the time. I don't even really think about it to be honest."

A small whirlwind of anger swirled inside Mallory at the thought that young men still thought it was appropriate to call someone they believed to be fifteen years old 'fit'. While they might look like young women, they were still essentially children at that age.

"So, after Tai walked out of the restaurant at nine-thirty, did you see or hear from her again?"

Chloe's face tightened, and she blinked back tears. "No. The next thing I knew, she was dead. I hate that the last thing I ever said to her was something horrible."

"What was the relationship like between you normally?"

Chloe wiped her face and shrugged. "Good, I guess. She could be a bit bossy sometimes, but she had a way of making you feel special, you know. Like you were a more important person because you were the one she'd chosen to spend time with."

"Was she the one who suggested joining the website?"

Chloe glanced down at her hands and nodded. "She always had money. She was able to buy whatever she wanted when we went to get something to eat and not just pick something cause it happened to be what was on offer. She was forever wearing different outfits, and her makeup brands were always on point. I knew it wasn't like she came from money or anything, so one day I asked her how she could afford all this stuff, and she was all secretive. She gave this weird smile and said they were presents. I asked who from, but she wouldn't tell me."

"That must have changed, though," Mallory said.

"Yeah, just over a month ago she told me the truth."

"What did you think?"

Chloe considered the question for a moment. "I mean, initially, I think I was kind of horrified, but then Tai explained that she wasn't actually having sex with anyone—at least, not yet. All she was doing was being flirty and suggestive in messages and sending a few pictures, and men were sending her money for it."

"She hadn't met anyone in person at that point then?" By 'person', Mallory was really thinking about Craig.

But Chloe shook her head. "Not that she'd told me, no. She said it was easy money and if it got a bit weird at all, you could just block the guy, or else you could close your account. You didn't post your face or full name, so it wasn't as though they could track you down or anything."

"So you thought you'd give it a go?"

"Yeah, why not? It wasn't like I hadn't sexted or sent pics to boys anyway, and now I'd be getting paid for it. I figured that if I didn't like it, I'd just shut down my account, and there wouldn't be any harm."

Mallory wanted to ask Chloe if she found it strange or weird that they were older men searching for younger girls, but she wasn't there to judge the morality of it all. She needed to keep her questioning relevant.

"How long was it before Craig Penn contacted you?"

"He dropped into my DMs a couple of weeks ago."

"He was under the username *ArcanePenMan?*" Mallory asked.

"That's right. We exchanged a few messages, and I sent some photos."

"Did he send you any money?"

She bit her lower lip, pink colouring her cheeks. "Yes, a couple of hundred quid. Then I mentioned the username to Tai, and it all blew up. She said she'd been meeting him in person and that he should be exclusive to her now. I couldn't see why. The whole point of being on the site was to make money, and I was. I didn't want to cut him off just because she said so, and he didn't think he should have to stop messaging me either. That's when things started to get ugly."

"Between you and Tai, or between Craig and Tai?"

"Both," she admitted.

Mallory put her forearms on the table. "You understand we now have Craig under arrest for Tai's murder? He's currently being questioned by one of my colleagues."

"Yes, I understand. You think he did it, then?"

"We have to explore all possibilities."

Did she think Craig was capable of murdering a seventeen-year-old girl? No, she never would have thought he'd do something so terrible. She knew he was a bit of a player and that he liked a drink and was a bit irresponsible. She could easily imagine him online on one of those websites, though she found the fact he'd used one deliberately aimed to find teenage girls distasteful. But could she imagine him killing one of the girls? No. Of course, that didn't mean he was innocent. How well could they know their work colleagues? She was fully aware that even Ryan had had his demons to wrestle with over these past few years, and those were things he had never wanted to talk about. She'd kept her own secrets from her colleagues, as well, too embarrassed or ashamed to tell the truth, so she could hardly blame others for doing the same.

"Let's go over the day Tai died. You met her at the McDonald's, but what did you do after she left?"

"I wandered round town for a bit, and then I went home."

"What time did you go home?"

Chloe wrinkled her nose as she thought. "A bit before ten, I think."

"Was your mum home then?"

"Yes, she was. We didn't really talk, though. I just went to my room and went to bed. I'd been up early because of college and I was tired."

"And what happened when you woke up?" Mallory asked.

Chloe twisted her hands together. "My mum woke me up. She was in a big panic, telling me Tai was dead and I was in danger and that we needed to leave. So we packed a bag and left."

"Why did she think you were in danger? Had Craig threatened you?"

She shook her head. "Not directly, no."

Mallory angled her head. "Not directly? What does that mean exactly? You know, threats don't have to be physical. Abuse doesn't have to be violent. Words and implications can be just as powerful."

"He never said anything bad to me. He was always polite. Nice, even. Not like some of the men who contacted me on there. Some of them were really horrible, saying explicit stuff on the first message."

"But he never threatened you directly?" Mallory double-checked.

If Craig had never threatened Chloe, why had they felt the need to run?

"No. I knew Tai was upset that he'd messaged me. She told me that she'd threatened to expose him if he didn't give her extra money, and that he'd said he was going to tell everyone she was basically a prostitute. I told her I thought she was an idiot. She didn't like that. Her reputation meant everything to her."

"Did she give you the impression she thought Craig might hurt her?"

Chloe hesitated. "Well, no, but then someone threw her off the bridge."

"And you assumed it was him?"

"From what Tai said about their argument, who else could it be?"

"Why didn't you come to the police?" Mallory asked.

"Craig *is* the police. My mum said that if we tried to tell anyone what we thought might have happened it would get covered up, and then he'd be free to come for me and keep me quiet, too."

Mallory frowned. "Your mum said that?"

"Yes." She sniffed and wiped her eyes. "I had to tell her. When she came to me and said that Craig had killed Tai and we had to go, I told her everything I knew."

Something jarred inside Mallory, and she adjusted herself in her seat. "Let me just get this straight, you hadn't told your mum about Craig before then?"

"No."

"So how did your mother know what was going on?"

"She heard that Tai had gone missing and then that a body had been found. I guess her and Tai must have been talking. My mum has known Tai since we were little kids. We went to the same primary school together, and our mums used to be friends."

"That must have been a shock for your mum, finding out what the two of you had been doing online?"

Chloe nodded. "It was. She was absolutely furious and upset. I've never seen her that way before. She was crying and couldn't stop shaking. She really frightened me."

Mallory wanted to check something. "Just to clarify, you hadn't told your mum anything about the sugar babies site at that point?"

"No. She would have gone nuts if she'd known about it, and she did."

Something wasn't ringing quite true with Mallory. It was like trying to force the wrong piece of a jigsaw puzzle into a hole.

"Do you know when your mother spoke to Tai?"

"No, I don't. I assumed it was after she and I had that fight?"

"The one in McDonald's?"

"Yes."

Mallory was starting to wonder if Chloe hadn't been the last person to see Tai alive after all.

Had there been any record of a phone conversation happening between Faye and Tai on the night she'd died? No, there hadn't, but there had been one between Chloe and Tai.

"Did Tai call you after you got home that night?" Mallory asked. "I mean, after you'd had the argument in McDonald's?"

"No, I already told you. That was the last time I spoke to her."

Mallory slid a printout of Chloe's phone records across the table. "According to your phone records, she called you shortly after ten the night she died."

"She didn't. I was asleep by ten."

"That's not what the phone records say, and I'm afraid they don't lie, Chloe."

Mallory's pulse quickened, the pieces slotting into place. There were still things she needed to confirm, but she had a sinking feeling that Faye had taken her daughter and run for a completely different reason than she was frightened of Craig. Mallory needed to bounce these thoughts off Ryan, see what he made of them. Maybe she was going in completely the wrong direction, but she had the sense she wasn't.

Mallory said she was pausing the recording and then offered Chloe a smile. "Thought we could both use a break," she said. "Can I get you anything? Tea? Coffee? Water?"

"Can I have a coffee, please?"

"Absolutely. You going to be all right if I leave you here for ten minutes?"

"Yes, of course."

Chloe had the social worker with her, so it wasn't as though she was being left alone.

Mallory left the room. She was glad they'd had the sense not to interview the mother and daughter together. She went to the room where Ryan was watching the interviews remotely.

"Have you been listening?" she asked him. "What are your thoughts?"

"That something doesn't add up."

"I thought the same. Why did Tai tell Chloe's mother everything but didn't tell her own?"

Ryan folded his arms across his chest. "Was Tai trying to get back at Chloe for refusing to shut down her sugar babies account? Tai was jealous that Craig had sent Chloe a message, and then Chloe didn't take Tai's side when she told her about it. Could Tai have contacted Faye and told her everything as a way of getting back at Chloe?"

"It's possible."

"We're still missing an hour between her leaving McDonald's and the time it would have taken to walk to the bridge. Could she have seen Faye in person? Gone to their house, even?"

"Maybe," Ryan said. "But then why did she end up on the bridge?"

"Could Faye have convinced Tai to go there, maybe arranged to meet someone there—Craig, even—and turned up herself?"

"You think Faye might have killed Tai? Could it be her on the CCTV footage?"

Mallory exhaled. "It's a possibility. Then she panicked and ran, using Craig as an excuse as to why they needed to disappear. Chloe said her mother was furious and upset. Could part of her emotion have been down to the fact she'd just killed a girl? A friend of her daughter's?"

Ryan twisted his lips. "Before we go any further, I think we need to look more carefully into Faye's movements before Tai's death."

Mallory wanted to believe no mother would be capable of killing her daughter's friend, but she'd seen far worse during her time on the force.

"I agree. Something isn't adding up here, and we need to find out what."

Chapter Thirty-Five

Before going into the interview with Faye, Ryan took some time to go over all the details of the case again.

He scoured through the phone records and then the bank files, analysing every phone call and transaction. What was he missing? He noted one particular payment on the day Tai had died and paused on it for a moment, wondering if it was more significant than it had first appeared.

He brought up the post-mortem file, then called Nikki Francis.

"Sorry to call so early," he apologised.

They'd worked right through the night.

"No problem. I was up anyway. Planned to get a run in before work."

"You might have to skip it for today. I need you to check something for me."

"Of course. Whatever you need."

He told her what he'd found.

"I'll call you as soon as I know anything," she said.

"Thanks."

He finished up what he was looking through and then headed into the interview room where Faye Jennings was waiting with her solicitor.

"Sorry to keep you waiting," he said, throwing Faye Jennings what he hoped was a winning smile. "And apologies once more for interrupting your trip. We wouldn't have done it if it wasn't important."

"It is getting very late, or perhaps I should say early," the solicitor pointed out. "Maybe this can wait until tomorrow? My client has had a long journey."

Ryan took a seat. "I appreciate that, but this really can't wait. I'm sure Miss Jennings is anxious to help us with our enquiries, considering she knew the victim, Tai Moore."

Faye did look exhausted. "Yes, of course. I'll do whatever I can to help. Is Chloe okay?"

"She's fine. She's being well taken care of. Just so you're aware, I will be recording this interview for our records."

She nodded and stared down at her hands.

Ryan began the recording and ran through the usual questions at the start of an interview, as well as mentioning who was present and the time and their location. With that out of the way, he got down to business.

"How well did you know the victim, Tai Moore?"

Faye shrugged. "I knew her up until she was eleven, when the kids left primary school, and then I didn't know her at all."

"But she and your daughter were friends?"

"I suppose so, but I wasn't aware of this friendship until recently. They'd lost touch and only were reunited when they started college."

"What did you think of Tai?"

"I didn't think anything of her. I didn't know her."

Ryan didn't buy that. Everyone had an opinion of someone else, even if it was only someone they'd met for ten minutes.

"When would you say the last time was that you saw or spoke to her?" Ryan asked.

She screwed up her features as she thought. "It's been years. I honestly couldn't say exactly."

"So you didn't see or speak to her the night of her murder?"

"No, of course not." Her tone grew higher in pitch.

"Where were you the night of Tai's murder?"

Faye's shoulders tensed. "At home, with my daughter. You can ask Chloe the same. She saw me when she came in that evening."

Ryan offered her another smile, hoping to win her over. If she got defensive it would make his job that much harder. "That's right. I believe she did say the same."

Faye's shoulders dropped. "Yes, she would."

"Do you know the name Craig Penn?" he asked.

Her lips thinned. "Yes, though I wish I didn't."

"What do you know about him?"

"That he's the one responsible for killing Tai and that he got involved with my daughter, too."

"Through the site Searching Benefits dot com?"

"Yes."

Ryan's phone buzzed in his pocket, and he took it out and glanced at the screen. It was Nikki.

"Would you excuse me a minute? I need to take this." He spoke the time for the sake of the recording and said he was pausing it.

He stepped outside the room. "What have you got for me?"

He listened while she filled him in.

"That's great," he said. "Thanks for getting back to me so fast."

He ended the call and went back inside. "Right, where were we?" Ryan moved to a different line of questioning. "Why did you take your daughter and leave for Scotland less than an hour after Tai's body was discovered?"

"I was worried for my daughter. I knew Craig had threatened Tai, and now she was dead. Was I supposed to just sit around and wait for him to come for her?"

Ryan frowned. "How did you know it was Tai's body that had been found? Her name hadn't been released to the press yet."

"It was all over social media that the police, and a search and rescue team, were on the Clifton Bridge because a teenage girl's body had been found. I guess I put two and two together."

"You just assumed it was Tai? That's a pretty big assumption to make. There are almost half a million people who live in Bristol. I don't know how many of those half a million are teenage girls, but I'd say there are a fair few. So why did you believe it was Tai Moore so strongly, that you not only packed up your daughter, but you left your phones and laptops behind so they couldn't be traced, and you even went as far as exchanging your vehicle for one worth thousands of pounds less than the one you owned?"

"I was frightened Craig would be coming to get Chloe next. Her safety was worth whatever sacrifices I'd have to make."

"Chloe says she hadn't told you anything about the website before the morning Tai's body was found and you told her that you both had to leave."

Faye screwed up her lips, her gaze darting down. "She didn't. Tai told me."

"Oh?" Ryan raised an eyebrow. "I thought you said you hadn't spoken to her for years."

"I forgot about that one time. She called Chloe that night, but Chloe was asleep, so I answered the phone."

"She called before she died? Why?"

Faye folded her arms across her chest. "I don't know why she phoned Chloe, but she and Chloe had a fight. When I answered the phone instead of Chloe, she must have decided to take it as an opportunity to get Chloe in trouble, so she told me everything."

"And did it? You didn't confront Chloe about it that night?"

She shook her head. "No, I didn't. She was asleep. I wanted to take time to think over how I was going to approach it, but then the next morning I woke up and Tai was dead."

"Or did you arrange to meet Tai?" he suggested. "Maybe you promised to help her figure things out and instead you took advantage of the trust of a vulnerable girl."

"Vulnerable girl?" Her eyebrows shot up, her jaw dropping open. Scorn laced her tone. "She didn't phone for help. She wanted to drag Chloe's name through the dirt, just like she'd dragged Chloe down to her level by joining that fucking site. My Chloe was a good girl before Tai came back into her life."

"Isn't the real reason you ran because you'd killed Tai by pushing her off the bridge? You hadn't realised her body would be found so quickly, but when you learned that it had, you panicked and ran. You were just using Craig Penn's connection to this all as an excuse to stop your daughter asking any more questions or refusing to go with you. You made Chloe believe she had a murderous police officer hunting her down."

"No! It was one of your lot who killed her! Don't try to put it on me." Faye puffed herself up. "See, I knew this would happen. You're trying to make it look like I had something to do with her death when it was that sicko colleague of yours."

Ryan didn't rise to it.

"What were you doing the day Tai died, Faye?" he asked instead.

She relaxed slightly. "I had the day off. I went to the garden centre and bought some plants for the garden."

"So you were gardening?" he checked.

"Yes."

"What kind of plants did you buy?"

She seemed baffled by this line of questioning. "I don't know. A mixture of different flowers."

"Did you happen to have chrysanthemums in that mixture?"

Her gaze shifted from side to side. She was clearly wondering where he was going with this. "Umm...yes, I believe I did."

"And you had those flowers in your car?"

"Yes. I had to get them from the garden centre to my house."

"We tested your car for chrysanthemum pollen and found a significant amount," Ryan said.

Faye blinked. "So?"

"There was also chrysanthemum pollen on Tai's body, in particular, pollen particles on her upper arms where the person who pushed her over the side of the bridge grabbed her."

Faye went completely still, her face draining of colour. "What are you saying?"

"You said you didn't see Tai the day she died."

"I didn't."

"So how did pollen from your car get onto her skin? It was only a small amount, just a few grains, something that we would typically see from someone who has been touching the plants and then touched something else. It's called secondary transference."

Tears filled her eyes, and she shook her head. "I don't know, it could have come from anywhere."

"Not that kind of pollen. This chrysanthemum species is called 'Elspeth' and is considered very rare and as 'threatened in cultivation' by Plant Heritage. It's not native to our country, you see, and that exact species of flower can only be bought from a handful of garden centres in the country, one of which happens to be the one you visited the day Tai was murdered."

Her voice was a whisper. "It—it's just a coincidence."

Ryan continued. "You weren't at home with your daughter on the night Tai was killed, were you? You waited until Chloe got home and went up to her room, where she was already asleep. Then you just happened to answer the call from Tai on Chloe's phone and Tai told you everything. You were so horrified that you decided to take things into your own hands and arranged to meet her. You knew Chloe wouldn't hear you leaving or getting back, and you left to take on Tai."

The tears welled in her eyes and spilled down her cheeks.

Faye crumbled. "Even at primary school, Tai was a little bitch, always bullying Chloe, getting to choose who was her friend and who she could play with. I was relieved when her mother said they'd be going to different schools. But then Chloe started college, and there Tai was again. Chloe changed when she came back into her life. I couldn't believe it when I spoke to Tai again and she told me all about the website and the police officer she'd got involved with."

"Was DC Penn threatening Tai?" he asked.

Faye shook her head. "No, *she* was threatening *him*. She was telling him that if he didn't give her more money, then she'd expose him. But he obviously wasn't happy about it and said that he'd tell everyone she was selling herself for sex, so I guess they were in a bit of a stalemate. Tai realised she'd got herself into a situation, and I said I would help her. I've known her since she was a kid, and she trusted me."

"So you went to meet her and killed her?"

"She dragged my daughter into this sordid life. She poisoned her. I just saw her there, in that little red dress and too much makeup, looking like a fucking hooker, and I realised she wasn't going to change. She was going to carry on dragging Chloe down with her unless I did something to stop her." She covered her face with her hands. "I didn't plan it. I thought maybe I'd scare her a bit, threaten her, tell her to stay away from my daughter. I didn't mean to push her! I was just so angry with her."

Ryan exhaled and sank back. They had her.

There was no joy in hearing the confession.

One girl was dead, and now another was going to have to go into adulthood with her mother behind bars. What would happen to Chloe? She was almost eighteen. He hoped the grandparents would step in and help.

But he was relieved it hadn't been one of his own who'd killed Tai Moore, though there would still be scandal around Craig's involvement in the case. At least he hadn't murdered

Tai. Something like that would have shaken his team right to the core. It was the sort of thing that left a stain so bad, it was impossible to get out. He'd envisioned them breaking apart, for each of them to move to different departments to try to escape the taint that would have followed them. It wouldn't have mattered that none of them had any idea about Craig and what he was doing outside of work. People still would have talked. They've have wondered if any of them had been protecting him and had known exactly what he was capable of. It was almost impossible to shake something like that, even if, as his work colleagues, they had been completely naïve to it. Even that naivety would have caused questions—asking why none of them had realised what kind of person Craig really was. They should have known if they were working with a killer, especially considering what their jobs were.

As it was, Craig's involvement with the teenage girls still didn't look good—for any of them—but it was a scandal that would be far easier forgotten than if he'd been a killer.

Ryan cleared his throat. "Faye Jennings, you are under arrest for the murder of Tai Moore. You do not have to say anything. But, it may harm your defence if you do not mention when questioned something which you later rely on in court. Anything you do say may be given in evidence."

Faye burst into tears and covered her face with her hands. "I'm sorry, I'm so sorry. God, what have I done. How's Chloe going to cope with having a mother in jail? Oh God, oh God."

She was crying hysterically now, folded in half, still hiding behind her hands. Ryan could barely understand what she was saying, howling in her grief at what she'd done, the realisation of the future that now lay ahead of her. Maybe she was even crying for the girl whose life she'd stolen. A girl she'd once known as an innocent child.

It wasn't often Ryan felt sorry for a killer, but he found his heart clenching for Faye. But then he remembered how she'd done everything she could to hide her tracks and would have let one of his officers take the blame for Tai's death, and he strengthened his resolve.

He had done his job. Tai's mother would know exactly what had happened to her daughter.

Chapter Thirty-Six

Ryan was happy to go home, and by home, he didn't mean his sad little flat but back to his old house.

He grabbed food on the way, so Donna didn't have to think she had to feed him again. The last thing he wanted was to become a burden to her in any way. He wanted his presence in her life to ease some of the struggles she had, not add to them.

She opened the door to him and caught sight of his face. "Rough day?" She checked her watch. "Or should I say night?"

"Oh, you know. The usual."

"I heard one of your team was involved." She must have seen his expression. "Sorry, social media is all over it."

"Damn. That wasn't what I wanted."

"No, I bet it isn't." She took the food from him. "That smells good. You want some coffee with that?"

He was tempted to have something stronger, but he knew that wouldn't help anyone. The case might be closed, but the fallout of what Craig had done had barely started. He needed to be on the ball.

Donna made them a coffee each, and he divided the pastries and fruit onto plates. They carried it into the living room and ate in front of the television, though he couldn't stomach a lot of it. The case had left him with a bad taste in his mouth. Even though they'd got their man—or woman—it didn't feel like a win.

"This feels like old times," he said. "You and me, eating in front of the telly."

With his words came a pang of pain. Old times would have meant having Hayley here, too, most likely complaining because she didn't really like the pastries with custard or fruit inside them and only liked chocolate.

Was there ever going to be a time when her loss and their shared pain was something that drew them together again instead of feeling like a wedge to drive them apart?

Donna finished her mouthful and put down her plate. "Ryan, I think if we're ever going to make this work, we need to forget 'old times' ever existed. We need to put the past behind us, everything we've gone through over recent years. If we keep looking back, we're just pulling all that grief and resentment and anger into the future with us."

Ryan stiffened. "How can we not look back? If we're not, then we're basically saying that we're willing to forget Hayley."

She shook her head. "That's not what I'm saying at all. I just think we need a fresh start. Us being here"—she waved her hand around—"isn't good for us."

"You mean this house? What are you saying?"

"There are too many memories here. Yes, some of them are good, but a lot of them only hurt. I wonder if it's time to put this place on the market and find somewhere new."

He hadn't been expecting this at all. Where he'd been thinking of the possibility of moving back in, and them feeling like a family again, she'd been considering moving on.

There was so much about this place that reminded him of their daughter. It felt like a betrayal to think about selling up.

"Do—do you mean us buying a new place together?"

He didn't think he wanted to sell this house, but maybe he could get his head around it if it meant them becoming a committed couple again.

But she shook her head. "I don't think it would be a good idea, Ryan. Not yet. I thought we could see how things went between us with me being in a new property first. There's no reason to rush into things. I like my independence."

He couldn't pretend her words weren't like a punch to the gut. He hadn't had much of an appetite before anyway, but now it vanished completely.

The old Ryan would have thrown the rest of his meal away and stormed out of the house. A part of him still wanted to do that, but he'd told himself he needed to learn from his mistakes. No more hot-headed responses. Shit, it wasn't easy, though. But Donna had been through far more than he had, and he had to keep reminding himself of that. If she felt she wanted her independence, then he had to let her have it for as long as she desired, and make sure that he was the one she turned to when—or if—she decided she needed him again.

Losing the house, though, and all the memories it contained, that was harder to stomach. The thought of another family living within these walls, erasing all the moments Hayley touched, hurt him deep down.

"Maybe we can talk about it," he suggested.

She looked at him. "There isn't really anything to talk about, Ryan. I own this house now. Everything is in my name. I don't need your permission to sell it. If it's what I decide I want to do then I will."

"We don't even get to have a discussion?"

"Not really. Ultimately, it's my choice."

Was he wrong to feel like he deserved at least a conversation about this? Or was she completely in the right? It wasn't as though they'd made anything official about their relationship yet. Technically, they were still exes.

"I've upset you, haven't I?" she said.

"No, I'm fine. It's just been a rough day, and you caught me off guard." He paused for a moment, carefully trying to pick his words. "I guess I just can't imagine a world where I can no longer go into Hayley's old bedroom and see where she slept or stand in the garden where she took her first steps. It feels a bit like you want to wipe her out of our lives."

"You know I would never want to do that, but while you want to hold on to all those memories, I just find them triggering. It was such a horrific time in both our lives, I can't help but find myself thrown right back there every time I think of her. I always thought that time would make it less raw, but honestly, I don't think it's worked that way. I need something to change if I'm going to live with whatever time I have left."

Ryan reached out and took her hand. "What do you mean by whatever time you have left. Your cancer is cured, remember?"

"I know. And I know what the doctors have said, but it's hard to shift into the frame of mind that I'm well again. I guess maybe I just haven't accepted it yet, but right now, I feel as though I'm not existing for the future or even living for the day. I'm just frightened of what lies ahead and frightened that I might not be strong enough to go through this again."

"You don't know that you ever will have to go through it again."

She pressed her lips together and nodded. "The trouble is, my brain doesn't know that. I guess that's why I was thinking a new house might help me change my frame of mind."

How could he possibly argue with that? How could he ask her to live with ghosts and a fear of dying?

He couldn't.

Her coffee mug was empty, so he picked it up. "Another?"

She smiled gratefully. "Thanks, Ryan. And thanks for being so understanding about this. I was worried about how you might react."

He didn't say anything to that but took her cup back into the kitchen and did his best to bury his feelings deep.

JOURNALISTS WERE OUTSIDE the station waiting for him when he went back to work the following morning. He'd expected it, but it was a shock, nonetheless, to be barraged by a volley of questions. He had to push through them all, saying, "Excuse me, excuse me," as he went. They shouted at him, asking questions all over the top of one another.

"Did you know about one of your detective's involvement with young girls?"

"Don't you think you *should* have known, DI Chase?"

Ryan put his head down and kept going. They had a media team who would be put in place to make a statement and handle any difficult questions. They were trained for this kind of thing, so it was better to leave it up to them.

There was a strange atmosphere in the office. Subdued. Where people would be ribbing each other and telling jokes—often ones that balanced on the line of bad taste—this morning everyone was quiet. They almost weren't meeting each other's eye, as though the poor actions of one officer had now left everyone in doubt of their colleagues and what secrets they might be hiding.

Ryan knew he had to bring everyone together again. In their job, they needed to know they could trust each other implicitly.

His phone rang, and he took the call. His heart sank as he listened to the CPS solicitor on the end of the line.

"I'll pass on the news," he said and ended the call.

Mallory came into the office. She looked thinner and more fragile than he was used to seeing her, and his stomach twisted at the knowledge that he was going to have to deliver some bad news. He wished things could have been different.

"Can I have a word?" he asked.

"Yes, of course. What's up?"

"Take a seat."

He thought she might give him an argument about not sitting down, but she dropped into the chair, though remained bolt upright, her palms pressed primly into her lap.

"The court decided there were no grounds for remand, so Daniel is out. There's a restraining order on him that he's not allowed to come within one hundred feet of you, but otherwise, he's out until his court date."

She paled, even more than she normally was. Her lips tightened. "It's what I expected, but it's still hard to hear. Now I'll be expecting to see him standing on my doorstep or waiting by my car every time I go home."

"He knows not to come near you, or he'll be straight back behind bars."

Mallory gave a small smile, but it didn't touch her eyes. "Yeah, how many times have we heard that before only for a man to go on to murder his partner?"

"Do you believe him capable of that?"

She closed her eyes for a moment and then opened them again and met his gaze. "I want to say no, but I'd never thought he was capable of locking me in a fucking cupboard either." A tear escaped the corner of her eye, and she swiped it away. "I'm worried that he might try something with Ollie, too. Oliver is so much more forgiving than me. I've told him that we can't speak to Daniel any more, but if Daniel tried to, and said all the right things, I can't say for sure that Ollie wouldn't go with him or even let him into the house."

"Take some time off," Ryan suggested. "Have a break. Take Oliver away for a bit."

She shook her head. "It's not that easy. You need me here, especially now we're one man down."

"We'll manage. Your safety and peace of mind is more important. Go and stay with your mum and dad for a while."

She gave a small laugh. "They'd never cope, even with me there."

Ryan thought of something. "Look, I have a flat that's mostly standing empty. You and Oliver are more than welcome to it for a while if it helps you feel safer. I'm sure Donna wouldn't mind if I move in for a short while, at least until Daniel's court date comes around."

He wasn't quite sure how true that was, but it felt like the right thing to do.

"Are you just using this as an excuse to move back into the house?" She gave him a smile, and it was real this time.

"You may have seen right through me on that one."

Donna wasn't going to be selling up anytime soon. Maybe if he could show her that things would still be good between them with him living there, she'd change her mind about everything. It would take months between putting the house on the market and her actually selling. She could think of it like a trial run.

She arched an eyebrow. "And don't you think Donna will, too?"

"Hmm, quite possibly, but I am serious about the offer. If it'll help you feel safer..."

She sighed. "Thanks. I appreciate the offer, I really do, but it would feel too much like running. That's our home, and it's where Oliver feels the safest and most comfortable. I don't want that arsehole chasing us out of there. It would make me feel like he'd won, you know. That I'd be admitting I'm frightened of him. I don't want that. I want to think of him like the pathetic loser bully that he really is, not someone I'd change my whole life over."

"I understand. As long as you're sure. And if you do ever change your mind, the offer is still open, okay?"

"Okay."

The rest of his team filtered into the office for the morning briefing. They were one man down, because of Craig being suspended, and it was highly unlikely he'd work on the force again. Even with Craig being innocent of murder, they couldn't afford to have that kind of dirt tainting their good name. He was fully aware that the others would have to step up to cover Craig's workload. In a way, it was good that Mallory didn't take that time off, as they couldn't really afford not to have her working either. He still worried about her, though. The thought of Daniel being out there, frightening her, made him want to find the little prick and break his legs himself. He knew he couldn't do such a thing—not without losing his job and serving time himself—but the desire lingered.

They'd discuss how to handle any questions that came their way about Craig. The media were like vultures. One wrong word from any of them, and they would leap on it and tear it to shreds. They had the ability to warp things to fit their own narrative. Not that anything that had happened needed to be warped. The truth was bad enough.

Before Ryan could get started, his mobile rang. "DI Chase."

"This is Sergeant Joslin. I've got a case I'd like you to take a look at."

No rest for the wicked, or was it that the wicked didn't rest?

"No problem," Ryan said. "I'll be right there."

About the Author

M K FARRAR HAD PENNED more than twenty novels of psychological noir and crime fiction. A British author, she lives in the countryside with her three children and a menagerie of rescue pets.

When she's not writing—which isn't often—she balances out all the murder with baking and binge-watching shows on Netflix.

You can find out more about M K and grab a free book via her website, https://mkfarrar.com

She can also be emailed at mk@mkfarrar.com. She loves to hear from readers!

Also by the Author

DI Erica Swift Thriller
The Eye Thief
The Silent One
The Artisan
The Child Catcher
The Body Dealer
The Mimic
The Gathering Man
The Only Witness
The Foundling

Detective Ryan Chase Thriller
Kill Chase
Chase Down
Paper Chase
Chase the Dead

Crime After Crime
Watching Over Me
Down to Sleep
If I Should Die

Standalone Psychological Thrillers
Some They Lie
On His Grave

Down to Sleep

Printed in Great Britain
by Amazon